His eyes were on hers
was not real.

His brain was already busy processing what little information she had been able to give him. He put the pen down on the desk.

"There's something else I need to know," he said. "Is there any chance, any chance at all, that the killer may have seen you?"

Julia shook her head. "I don't think so, he took off straight away."

"That doesn't necessarily mean he didn't see you," he said slowly.

Julia blanched and fisted her hands in her lap. "I know it doesn't, Inspector," she said curtly, "but isn't it your job to reassure me? Make me feel safe?"

He didn't answer, just continued to stare at her while methodically rubbing his hand back and forth along his jaw.

Julia crossed her arms. "Well?"

A flicker of something flashed behind his eyes as he watched her. Julia frowned. *Doubt? Suspicion? No...wait a minute...was that amusement?*

"Why are you looking at me like that?" she demanded. "Don't you believe me?"

"I believe you, it's just I've never come across such open hostility from a civilian before, that's all," he said, a small smile playing at the corners of his mouth. "Do you have a problem with just me or cops in general?"

Reluctant Witness

by

Rachel Brimble

To / Julia,

I hope you enjoy your
namesake's story!

Rachel
Brimble
x.

Reluctant Witness

Contact Information: info@thewildrosepress.com

Cover Art by *Kim Mendoza*

The Wild Rose Press
PO Box 706
Adams Basin, NY 14410-0706
Visit us at www.thewildrosepress.com

Publishing History
First Crimson Rose Edition, 2008
Print ISBN 1-60154-341-7

Published in the United States of America

Dedication

To Jessica & Hannah—
the girls who are the light of my life.
I love you.
xxx

Chapter One

Julia Kershaw pulled her Volkswagen Beetle to a stop in the beach parking lot and killed the engine. With the afternoon to herself and the July temperature at a warm seventy-eight degrees, all she had planned was an afternoon relaxing in her private Cove. She stuffed a half-read paperback, sunglasses and binoculars into her handbag before making her way down the steps and over the soft golden sand. The salty smell of the sea momentarily swept away her anxiety and made her smile.

The sounds of the jet-skis and children playing descended into relative silence as she strolled farther and farther along the beach until she was completely alone. She climbed over several sun-baked boulders and jumped into her own special space, where no one would find her.

She slipped the leather flip-flops from her feet and sat in the sand. The ocean ebbed and flowed calmly beneath the sunshine, the beauty of the water shone with diamonds and fluffy white waves. Shielding her eyes from the sun, Julia contemplated a solitary boat way out on the English Channel as it lazily bobbed on the surface. A perfect day for sailing—or Julia's preferred option right now—topping up the tan.

She pulled her binoculars from her bag. The boat was too far out for her to make out the faces of the two men standing at the helm, but the way they were squaring up to each other spelled trouble. She fiddled with the focus on her binoculars but couldn't see them any clearer.

The heavier of the two wore a flamboyant

printed shirt tucked into knee-length navy shorts, his grey hair thin on top and a little bushier at the sides. Julia chewed her bottom lip as she tried to figure out why he looked so familiar.

The guy with him was an entirely different matter. Average height and slightly effeminate in his stance, he reminded Julia of her Uncle Charlie who had recently eloped with another man, causing her father to have a near cardiac arrest. Despite the sun's heat, he was dressed entirely in black from the cap covering his hair to his baggy jeans. Julia grimaced. The arrogant tilt of his chin, told her he was vain enough to crack a mirror. She was just about to turn away when Mr. Conceited put a hand to something at the back of his pants and held it there.

Julia narrowed her eyes but still couldn't make out what it was. Using his free hand, he pointed toward the shore. The man in the shorts turned to follow the direction of his finger. That was when Julia's blood turned cold. The man in black pulled the something from his pants—and the something looked very much like a gun. He raised it high and aimed it at the back of the other man's head.

"What the hell...?" Julia's heart leapt into her throat and perspiration broke out on her forehead as she clasped a hand to her mouth.

My God, he's going to shoot him, right here, right now! I've got to do something. Call for help, ring 911. . ?

She dropped the binoculars and desperately searched for her phone inside her bag.

Where is it? Panicking, she looked back to the boat and froze. The shot was nothing more than a muffled bang—nothing distinct, nothing that would cause any attention. The victim's body jerked hard and his arms flew back before he toppled backward onto the deck. Julia grappled for her binoculars once more. She watched with a thumping heart as the man in black stuffed the gun into his belt and leaned down to where the other man had fallen. The binoculars shook in Julia's trembling hands.

"Oh God, oh God."

Julia muttered the words over and over as she watched a cold-blooded killer heave and shove the dead man over the side of the boat. She saw a splash before the body slid into its liquid coffin.

Julia remained perfectly still, terrified to move. What if the man with the gun looked across the water and spotted her, sitting alone in her hidden cove?

He would kill her, track her down and kill her.

After what felt like a hundred years, the boat finally roared to life and took off. Julia exhaled in a rush and frantically shook everything out of her bag. Her phone wasn't there. Cursing, she remembered leaving it on her Mom's dining room table earlier that day.

She threw her belongings back into her bag and raced from the Cove. The last thing she wanted was go to the police station but knew she had no choice. Of all the times to be drawn into another killing in Corkley Park.

She pulled to a stop outside the police station, got out and ran up the stone steps, taking them two at a time. The lobby was deserted. Disregarding protocol, she strode straight past the front desk to the back offices, where she plowed through the door marked Detective Inspector. As it crashed against the wall announcing her arrival, Julia froze.

The man who stood behind Inspector Langton's desk with his hand hovering over the butt of the gun holstered at his hip was not the elderly, seaside detective she had been expecting. It was someone else entirely.

"Miss? Are you all right?" he asked, carefully. "Is

there some sort of problem here?"

Julia opened her mouth but nothing came out. His startled eyes were the deepest, darkest chocolate-brown and his hair as black as night.

She swallowed. "What?"

His hand didn't leave the gun. "Are you all right?"

She couldn't drag her eyes from his. "Yes, yes, no, not really."

"Are you looking for someone?"

She shook her head and refocused. "Detective Inspector Langton. I need to speak to him. Something's happened, something terrible. I..." Her voice cracked and she couldn't stop the tears that sprang into her eyes. "Oh, God."

The man moved his hand from the gun as he closed the gap between them. His fingers lightly touched her shoulder. "Why don't you come and sit down? You're really pale."

She let him steer her toward his desk and sank gratefully into the visitor's chair. "Thank you."

"You're welcome. Would you like a drink of water?"

Julia shook her head.

"Why don't you tell me what's happened?" he asked, gently. "Did someone at the front desk send you in here?"

"No, there's no one out there. I just came straight in," Julia said, looking away from his concerned gaze and straightening her shoulders, suddenly feeling conscious of every part of her body. "Look, I'm sorry but I just need to speak to Inspector Langton. Can you tell me where he is?"

He leaned a hip against the desk. "He's taken retirement."

"He has? But I need to talk to him urgently."

He held out a hand, a small smile lifting the corners of his mouth. "Maybe I can help. I'm the new

DI. Daniel Conway. Please to meet you, Miss...?"

She snapped her head up to look at him. "You're the new DI? But that's impossible."

He arched an eyebrow and let his hand drop. "Oh? Why's that?"

"You're...you're..."

Too bloody gorgeous to be a police officer for a start.

"A bit young to be a DI," she said, instead.

He laughed, the sound warm and entirely masculine. "I'm thirty-two but thanks for the compliment."

A sudden heat warmed her cheeks. "It wasn't meant as a compliment," she snapped.

He held his hands up. "OK, wow. Well, I moved here three weeks ago and took over Ed's position," he said, but Julia noticed a tightening in his jaw, before he seemed to visibly relax. "Look, Miss...?

"Kershaw. Julia Kershaw."

"Look, Miss Kershaw, why don't you tell me what brought you here?"

"You don't sound too pleased about that."

"About what?"

"About taking over from Ed." Was it possible that Corkley Park's new DI was about as happy to be in this office as she was?

"I'll ask you again," he said, ignoring her observation. "What brought you crashing into my office?"

She straightened her shoulders and met his gaze. *Touchy, touchy, Inspector. Cops. One rule for them, another for the rest of us.*

She blew out a breath. Common sense told her this was not the time to vent her frustration with the whole damn lot of them. A man was dead. A man she still swore she knew.

"OK, there's no easy way to explain this, so I'll just go ahead and say it. I just saw a man shot and thrown into the ocean. There was nothing I could do to stop it and I don't even know if anyone else saw it. I came straight here."

His cocoa eyes darkened. "You've just witnessed a murder?"

"Yes, at the beach. Well, not the beach. There's a Cove, a small inlet that can't be seen from the beach. The boat was out on the water and one man just shot another stone dead, and then pushed him overboard."

"And this happened when?"

"Less than half an hour ago. I came here straight away, I didn't know what else to do." Her voice began to rise with each word.

"OK, OK, it's all right. You're going to be fine." He pushed himself away from the desk and dropped to his haunches in front of her. A breeze of sandalwood teased her nostrils. Ignoring the unexpected kick in her chest, Julia tried to concentrate.

"You need to tell me everything just as you remember it," he said.

She swallowed. "There's not much to tell. I was sitting on the sand and noticed this boat way out on the water. I picked up my binoculars—"

"You saw their faces?"

"No, they were too far out. I can tell you what the guy with the gun was wearing but I wasn't close enough to describe him apart from his build. He was wearing a cap that covered his hair and I think he had sunglasses on too."

The Inspector stood and walked around the desk to his chair. He sat, took out a pen and paper, and looked at her expectantly. "Tell me what you can."

Julia closed her eyes and told him everything she could remember about the shooter.

"The man who was shot...he seemed familiar to me but I have no idea why."

"Could he have been a local resident?"

"I suppose it's possible."

"What about the boat itself?"

She blew out a breath. "It was white with a lot of chrome, I don't know anything about boats. There was nothing different or particular that caught my eye."

"Nothing at all? Name, shape?"

She opened her eyes. "Everything happened so fast. One minute I was thinking how much I would like to be on a boat like that, the next, one of the men had pulled out a gun."

His eyes were on hers but Julia could tell his mind was not really seeing her. His brain was already busy processing what little information she had been able to give him. He put the pen down on the desk.

"There's something else I need to know," he said. "Is there any chance, any chance at all, that the killer may have seen you?"

Julia shook her head. "I don't think so, he took off straight away."

"That doesn't necessarily mean he didn't see you," he said slowly.

Julia blanched and fisted her hands in her lap. "I know it doesn't, Inspector," she said curtly, "but isn't it your job to reassure me? Make me feel safe?"

He didn't answer, just continued to stare at her while methodically rubbing his hand back and forth along his jaw.

Julia crossed her arms. "Well?"

A flicker of something flashed behind his eyes as he watched her. Julia frowned. *Doubt? Suspicion? No...wait a minute...was that amusement?*

"Why are you looking at me like that?" she demanded. "Don't you believe me?"

"I believe you, it's just I've never come across such open hostility from a civilian before, that's all," he said, a small smile playing at the corners of his mouth. "Do you have a problem with just me or cops in general?"

Julia was on her feet in a instant. She hitched her bag onto her shoulder. "If we're finished here, *Inspector,* I'll leave you to it."

She turned toward the door.

"I'm sorry, Miss Kershaw, but you can't go anywhere yet."

She swiveled round to face him. "That's where you're wrong, Inspector. I can do what the hell I like. You've got no right..."

He reached for the phone on his desk. "The first thing we need to do is get that body out of the water. I'll get the troops down there, ready to meet us."

"Us?" Julia stared at him, floored. "What do you mean us?"

"I'm sorry but you're going to have to show me exactly where you were when you saw all this happen."

And as he spoke into the phone, Julia tipped her head back and squeezed her eyes shut. *How the hell had this happened?* One minute she was in her mother's kitchen, talking about leaving Corkley Park, the next she was embroiled in a murder investigation. Could fate be any more cruel?

"Julia? Are you all right?"

She dropped her head, opened her eyes and sighed. "What would you do if I said no?"

He didn't answer.

"Exactly," she said. "Your car or mine?"

He smiled and Julia felt her stomach tilt. "We'll take mine," he said. "After all, I'm the one with a siren and flashing blue light."

****

Julia wrapped her arms tighter around herself as she watched the scene unfold in front of her. Feeling more than a little redundant, she watched in

8

silence as Inspector Conway issued instructions left and right to the mass of people treading heavy footprints all over her precious cove. The space had been cordoned off with blue and white tape and as it snapped against the steadily rising breeze, Julia's anxiety rose along with it.

"At last," the new DI said, joining her at the shore. "The troops have arrived."

She jumped. "Pardon?"

"The troops. They've arrived."

She looked out across the water, following the direction of his outstretched finger. Up ahead, more or less in the exact spot where the killer's boat had been, a black and yellow police boat bobbed on the waves. She pursed her lips tightly together as the divers pulled on their wetsuits and flippers.

"Are you sure they're in the right place?" he asked.

"Uh-huh."

"Definitely? I can always speak to them via radio if needs be."

She lifted her chin to meet his gaze. "That's where he threw him in. Right there."

He nodded before turning back to the boat. Speaking into his hand-held radio, he said, "Go ahead."

Julia watched the divers leap overboard and into the water. Nothing remained for her to do now but wait to see who they brought to the surface.

"Are you OK?" His smooth, masculine voice cut through her thoughts.

She turned to look at him and the compassion in his eyes caught her completely off guard.

"I'm fine," she began, but then she was slowly shaking her head from side to side. "No. No, I'm not."

He reached out and gently gripped her elbow, leading her away from the rest of the assembled group. "Come and sit down," he said, easing her onto

9

one of the many boulders scattered around the edge of the Cove. "It isn't much in the way of comfort but at least you won't have so far to fall if you pass out."

She managed a smile at that. He'd said it as though he believed she might crumple to the ground any minute. If only he knew how much she'd had to deal with over the last six months. This was just another challenge God had obviously saw fit to bestow on her. She blew out a breath.

"I'll be fine."

"People have passed out over a lot less, believe me."

She turned away from him. "Is that so?"

"Different things affect different people. I've known a cat stuck in a tree to make one old woman pass out, you wouldn't believe—"

Julia rolled her eyes. "Well bully for them but I'm not most *people*, Inspector. Trust me. I will not pass out."

She could feel his stare boring into her temple but refused to look at him. He picked up a stray twig from the sand. "You really don't like me, do you?"

"That's neither here nor there under the circumstances."

"Fair enough."

She inhaled deeply. "Do you have any idea how quickly your life can be turned on its axis in one moment?" she asked, quietly.

She heard him exhale. "Unfortunately in my line of work, I know only too well how a moment in time can change a person's life forever," he said. "One minute..."

"This is such bad timing," Julia muttered.

"Is there ever a good time to witness a murder?"

Julia pressed her thumbs against her closed eyelids. "God, did I really just say that? I didn't mean..."

His fingers unexpectedly circled her wrist and

she flinched as his thumb pressed into the bruise there.

"Hey, sorry, did I hurt you?" he asked. But instead of dropping her arm, he turned it over. Julia's heart thumped hard behind her ribcage.

Shit. Here we go. She tilted her chin defiantly. He stared at the mark for a long moment before opening his mouth to speak, but Julia yanked her arm from his grasp and stood, stepping away from him before he had the chance to form any words.

"So...what happens now?" she asked, looking out over the water with her back toward him. She heard his shoes shift in the sand but didn't need to turn around to know he stood close behind her. The scent of sandalwood and fresh air settled around her like a cocoon. She resisted the temptation to breathe a little deeper as he lingered a while longer before moving to her side.

"We wait here until they bring up whatever they find down there," he said, quietly.

She nodded. "OK. We wait, then."

Julia kept her gaze firmly fixed on the water as the next few seconds beat out uncomfortably loud between them.

"Miss Kershaw? Julia? Can I ask you something?"

She didn't turn around. "If it's about what I saw this afternoon, yes you can, but if it's about the mark on my wrist...no you can't."

"Julia..."

She let out a dry laugh and tipped her head up to look at him. "Oh, I see, it's Julia now. What's this? You've slipped further into caring cop mode now, is that it?"

His jaw tightened and Julia found herself struggling to meet his angry gaze but refused to look away.

"If you don't want to tell me how you sustained

11

that injury, that's your business," he said. "I won't force you to tell me anything you don't want to."

"Too right, you won't," she retorted. "Because I won't let you."

"But as a police officer I am here to help you if I can."

She smiled slowly. "I'm fine, Inspector. Apart from witnessing a man being killed today. That, of course, is a bit of a problem but fortunately you are right here, on hand, to solve that problem."

His gaze met hers for a moment longer. "You're absolutely right."

And then he swept past her. His absence made her shiver. Feeling incredibly foolish and more than a little childish, Julia stumbled after him, cursing. Not only had she witnessed a murder, she now had the town's highest ranking police officer wanting to ask questions about the stupid bruise on her wrist. The fact that Marcus, her ex, was becoming a royal pain in the ass had nothing to do with DI Conway.

The sooner she got out of town the better.

****

Fifteen minutes later, Julia was shielding her eyes against the lowering sun as the police boat sped along the water toward them. When it moored at the edge of the pier, she couldn't pull her eyes away from the black body bag lying behind the officers on board. She trembled as they lifted it from the boat and laid it carefully onto the pier's planks.

The sound of the zipper being lowered grated on her nerves as she struggled to regulate her breathing. She purposely stood a few feet away, her gaze hovering above, below and to the side of the body—anywhere to avoid looking directly at it. She heard Inspector Conway address a member of his team.

"Well? Do you recognize him? Is he local?"

A long pause. "Yes, sir. He is. He owns a

convenience store on the High Street."

Julia's heart began to race. She knew nearly every store owner in town. She bit down on her bottom lip as both the young officer and Inspector Conway rose to their feet.

"His name is Derek Palmer, sir," the young officer said.

Julia rushed forward, pushing past Inspector Conway. "No, it can't be. Derek? Derek!" She saw the dead man lying at her feet and slapped a hand to her mouth. "No, no, no. Oh, God, Derek. Close it, close it!"

Without thinking, she turned and buried her head against Inspector Conway's chest. His arms came around her, strong and unyielding. Derek's pale, grey face loomed distinct and clear behind her closed eyelids.

"I'm so sorry, Julia," the Inspector said softly against her hair.

She shivered involuntarily. Fighting the urge to stay where it suddenly felt safe, Julia moved out of his arms and forced herself to stand upright. "He was such a lovely man. I don't understand," she said, tears burning her eyes. "He opens the store as regular as clockwork. Six o'clock every morning. Never asks for anything, always minds his own business. Why would someone want him dead?"

He gently cupped her elbow and moved her farther down the pier. Shock engulfed her body and ice-cold perspiration broke out along her spine. The slow transition of emotions flowed through her body. Shock gave way to disbelief, which gave way to grief, which finally gave way to anger. Derek was dead, and if she left it to the police, his killer would more than likely walk away a free man.

Abruptly she turned to face the man in charge. "You have to find his killer, Inspector. Promise me you'll find him." Her voice cracked. "You have to make sure he's locked away for the rest of his sorry, sick, spiteful life. Do you understand me?"

"I'm going to do all I can to find..."

She lifted a hand when he moved to touch her. "That's not good enough. You're the detective, you need to find out who did this and why. I'm just glad Inspector Langton isn't here to see this. Derek was one of his closest friends."

She brushed her hair back from her face. "God knows what this will do to him when he finds out. As for..." She stopped.

"What? What is it?" Conway asked, his hand still hovering close to her elbow.

His handsome face blurred through her tears. "Thelma. His wife. She's going to be devastated. She'll never get over this. They've been happily married for nearly forty years."

He glanced back at the body bag, which was being lifted into a van to be transported to the morgue. Slowly, he turned back to face her. "Listen, why don't you go home and I'll come by later to speak to you again?" he said, pulling a notepad and pen from his back pocket. "What's your address?"

"Why do you want me to leave now?"

"Because your face is white, you look scared and..."

"When will you be telling Thelma?" she demanded. "I need to be there. She can't have a stranger coming to her door with the news that her husband has been murdered. I can't let her go through that alone. No way."

"I'll be going to see her as soon as I leave here. But you cannot accompany me..."

"The only place I'm going, Detective is with you to see Thelma," said Julia. "I'm sorry but I couldn't care less if you have a problem with that."

He studied her for a moment before his jaw tightened once more. "Is that so? Well, for your

14

information, I *do* have a problem with civilians telling me what part they are going to play in *my* investigation, but if you feel you have a viable reason why you should come with me, I'm willing to listen."

Julia swiped a tear from her cheek. "Look, I'm sorry to yell but you have to understand Thelma and Derek were inseparable. They loved each other like no other couple I know. Please. You have to let me do this. She shouldn't be alone when you tell her he's dead."

He shook his head. "It isn't appropriate."

"Please, Daniel...I mean, Inspector, don't do this."

His eyes wandered over her face, before he blew out a breath. "Don't do what? My job?"

"Don't deliver the news to her like it's an everyday occurrence. It's the worst possible thing to hear it said like that."

"I am not going to..."

"Can't you just show a bit of empathy? There has to be one cop on this earth with a heart."

"What's that supposed—?"

She held up a hand. "It's just...look, please, let me come with you."

His eyes held hers for a long moment before he held his hands up in surrender. "Fine, you can come. You've got spunk, Julia. It's—an admirable trait."

He walked past her, heading for his car and Julia narrowed her eyes at his retreating back. For a second, she'd thought his observation was meant as a compliment but then she'd seen that damn twitching at the corners of his mouth.

Chapter Two

Daniel held the car door open for her and she slid into the seat. From the way she hesitated, her brow creased in confusion, Daniel had the distinct impression she wasn't often exposed to old-fashioned gallantry. Well, while in his company she might as well get used to it. Julia Kershaw was a lady and he would treat her as such.

"Are you OK?" he asked, leaning on the open car door.

"As well as can be expected under the circumstances," she muttered, reaching for the handle.

Daniel smiled. "Allow me."

He waited until she'd put her hand back in her lap before closing the door. He made his way around to his side of the car, got in and reached for his seatbelt. They had not found one other person at the beach who had taken any notice of the boat, so Julia Kershaw had quickly become the sole witness to Derek Palmer's murder.

And that worried him.

With no guarantee the killer hadn't seen her, it became an extremely dangerous situation for Julia. Daniel would be keeping a close eye on her until he had Derek's killer safely behind bars. A fact he was sure she would welcome about as much as a tooth extraction without anesthetic.

He gunned the engine and glanced at Julia. He took in the determined set of her jaw and the way her head was resolutely turned toward the window. A smile rose inside him. Something about this woman sent his stomach spinning and his mind reeling. But he could not allow himself to become distracted from the fact that she was his most crucial link in the investigation.

Why her open hostility toward the police? Surely she knew he would do everything in his power to catch Derek's killer and protect her?

Turning back to the windshield, Daniel pulled out of the beachside parking lot. His officers had tried reaching Thelma Palmer, but she wasn't answering her phone. They had no choice but to trawl all over town until they found her. She could be anywhere. Corkley Park was the kind of place where people still dropped in on neighbors for a cup of coffee, gave a helping hand at a jumble sale or simply decided to spend the day sitting outside one of the numerous cafes watching the world go by.

Julia gave a heavy sigh beside him.

"You OK?" he asked.

"Fine."

She didn't turn to face him and his smile returned. She was a feisty one, he had to give her that. When she'd stormed into his office, more or less taking the door off its hinges, Daniel had leapt to his feet, readying himself for some sort of ambush. Instead, it had taken all his strength not to let out a wolf whistle. To say Julia Kershaw was beautiful was a massive understatement.

Her hair was sunshine blond, thick and curly, and fell a few inches below her shoulders—-a perfect frame to showcase her intelligent, curious face. Her figure? He shifted in his seat as his pants became tighter. It was good to see at least one woman left on this earth that leaned more toward Marilyn Monroe than Twiggy.

"What's so funny, Inspector?"

Her voice broke through his sudden discomfort.

"Pardon me?"

He met those big green eyes for an instant before turning back to the road.

"You were smiling. I'm interested to know what you could possibly be smiling about when we're on our way to tell a woman her husband has been shot dead and his body just hauled out of the ocean."

He kept his eyes facing front. She was right. "I wasn't smiling, Miss Kershaw, I was thinking."

"You were smiling."

His grip tightened on the steering wheel. "I was thinking."

"You were smiling and I want to know when murder became so amusing to you. I'm sure you've seen more dead people than I've had hot dinners but that is no excuse—"

He swung the car to the curb and killed the engine. He swiveled around in his seat. "Enough! I wasn't smiling. Now, just drop it."

She narrowed her eyes. "How dare you—"

"We are going to see Thelma Palmer, and when we get there you're going to let me get on with doing my job. Is that clear?"

She crossed her arms. "Do you always speak to witnesses like this?"

"No, but I don't get many witnesses who actually speak to me the way you are, either."

Their eyes locked. Bronze. The flecks in her eyes were bronze. The observation seeped into his mind before he could stop it. He shook his head. "Look, are we done here? Because I refuse to waste any more time in a battle of wills with you. I've got a murder to solve."

She glared at him for a moment longer. He waited. Slowly her shoulders relaxed and her chin lowered. "Maybe I shouldn't have shouted at you," she said. "I've got a lot going on at the moment and witnessing the killing of one of the nicest people to walk this earth is just about as much as I can take."

He quietly exhaled. "Is it anything you want to talk about?"

"No."

"Are you sure?" He couldn't help a glance toward the bruising on her wrist.

She covered it with her hand and when he met her eyes again, her gaze was steely. "Yes. Completely sure. Shall we go?"

He blew out a breath. "Tell you what, why don't we call a truce? From now on there will be no more shouting, and more importantly, under absolutely no circumstances will there be any more smiling. Agreed?"

She eyed him suspiciously for a second or two, before her deliciously full lips slowly curved into a full-blown grin. The blood immediately rushed to the surface of Daniel's skin.

"Agreed," she said.

Giving her an encouraging wink, he swiveled back round in his seat and started the car. They traveled a few minutes in silence before he spoke again. "Thelma Palmer wasn't answering her phone earlier. One of my officers tried both her home number and her cell several times. Do you think she could be at the store?"

Julia looked at her watch. "It's almost six-thirty. She'll be at home preparing Derek's dinner." Her breath hitched. "Oh, God, this is going to destroy her."

"Listen to me. She'll get through this. It may take a year, it may take more, but in my experience, with support, people always get through losing a loved one."

Her face paled and her shoulders went rigid.

"Julia? Have I said something wrong?"

"A year, maybe more, huh? Is that the average grieving period—-in your experience?"

"I'm only saying..."

"Let's hope you're right. For all our sakes."

"What do you mean?"

She ignored the question. "Can I ask you something?"

He glanced at her. "Sure."

"I'm leaving town in less than two weeks on the Princess II..."

Daniel's stomach gave an inexplicable lurch at this news but he kept his face neutral as she continued.

"...And I have to be on that ship..."

"Have to be?" he asked.

"Yes, it's important."

"And you want to know how long this investigation to is likely to take?" He looked straight ahead, ignoring the rush of disappointment he felt. His gut instinct had told him Julia wasn't the type to think of herself first, but it turned out he'd been wrong. "I'm not sure. Could be days, could be months. I thought Derek Palmer was important to you."

"He is."

"So why the rush?"

"Because...because I've landed the most fantastic job and it could be the best career move of my life."

"I see."

"Don't say it like that. You don't know anything about me. I've worked hard for years and this is the first time an opportunity like this has come along."

"It's a job, Julia. We're talking about a life here."

She chewed her bottom lip before she turned away and looked out of the side window. She let out a wry laugh. "I don't know why I'm even justifying myself to you. What the hell do you know?"

They pulled to a stop at a set of traffic lights and he turned to look at her. "There you go again with the throw away comments. If you've got something to say, will you just say it?"

She crossed her arms but said nothing.

"I'm guessing your silence means there's more to your leaving," he continued. "Am I right?"

"Only a cop would have the nerve to ask that."

He smiled dryly before starting the engine once more. "Comes with the territory, I'm afraid."

****

The Palmer's cottage was situated on the outskirts of town in a pretty cul-de-sac. The window shutters and front door were painted a sunny yellow and the cottage's beautiful thatched roof completed its storybook appeal. The garden was as colorful as a painter's palette with strong pinks, blues, reds and purples scattered everywhere in a lovingly planted display of summer flowers. From the outside, it looked a happy household, but Daniel knew it was what went on inside a house that often solved a case.

He pushed open the gate and led the way up the path, but once they reached the door it was Julia who rang the bell.

He touched her arm. "I'll be taking the lead once we're inside."

"I know, Inspector. You've already made it clear I'm stepping on your toes."

Before he could answer, Mrs. Palmer's blurred silhouette appeared behind the door's glass panels. They turned to face her and when Daniel looked into Thelma Palmer's laughing eyes, the burden of his job weighed heavy on his chest. He was about to blow her entire life apart.

"Good evening, Mrs. Palmer. I'm Detective..."

But she wasn't looking at him. She was gazing at Julia with open adoration. She opened her arms and pulled Julia into a huge, motherly hug. "Oh, darling, it's so lovely to see you," she said, swaying Julia from side to side. "Where have you been hiding yourself for so long?"

21

Daniel watched Julia squeeze her eyes shut over Mrs. Palmer's shoulder but it didn't stop the tear escaping from beneath her lashes. "We need to go inside, Thelma," she managed. "We've got something to tell you."

"Well, sure, sweetie. Why don't you come on in? Both of you," she said, releasing Julia and gesturing for Daniel to follow them inside. "So are you Julia's new man? About time she had some strapping lad beside her."

Julia blew out a breath. "Thelma, for goodness sake. At least let the poor man inside before you start questioning him."

Thelma giggled. "I'm just waiting for Derek to get home. He's running late but that's all right, maybe we'll have time for a nice cup of tea before he starts hollering about an empty stomach, eh?"

As they followed her into the house, Daniel watched Julia brush the tears from her eyes with the back of her hand. But then she turned to look at him and pressed her fingers into his forearm.

"Please, let me do this," she said, urgently. "You saw how happy she is. This is going to devastate her."

"Julia, it's my job."

"I appreciate that. I do. It's just—"

Thelma poked her head through the kitchen door. "What are you two whispering about? Go into the living room and make yourselves comfortable. I'll bring some tea in."

Daniel let Julia steer him into the living room. Her fingers still gripped his arm. Once they were sitting down, she finally let go.

"Please, Daniel."

"Inspector."

She waved a dismissive hand. "Sorry, *Inspector*."

He tried not to smile at her sarcastic tone. The tiger was back out of its cage. "It's important I'm the one to tell her, Julia. I know how to handle situations like this. I'll be sympathetic. You'll just have to trust me."

"But this isn't about you, is it?" she whispered. "It's about Thelma. It should be me that tells her about Derek." She paused. "You're just a stranger."

Their eyes locked. Maybe her words weren't meant as a snub but they immediately made Daniel feel as though she would never accept him as a part of this town. He would forever remain an outsider to this exclusive circle of people.

Wasn't that what he wanted? He'd told his Chief a small town like Corkley Park was not where he should be. He was a city cop through and through.

He swallowed. "Thank you. It's nice to know how you see me."

He knew it was wrong to make her feel bad, but a wave of satisfaction swept through him to see her cheeks color. It was a spiteful thing for her to say and now at least, she knew it as well.

"I'm sorry, Inspector, I—"

Thelma bustled into the room, carrying a tray laden with a teapot, cups and biscuits. He watched Julia snap her mouth shut.

"Here we are," Thelma announced, as she placed the tray in front of them on a low table. "Who's for sugar?"

He tore his gaze from Julia's. "Mrs. Palmer, I'm Detective Inspector Conway. Can I ask that you sit down for a moment?"

"Inspector? But I thought you and Julia..." She slowly lowered herself into an opposite armchair, her wrinkled brow wrinkling further. "Is something wrong?"

Her eyes were already tearing up and Daniel's heart began to beat a little harder in his chest. He turned to face Julia, whose cheeks were now damp. "I think it best if Miss Kershaw tells you why we're

23

here. Miss Kershaw?"

Julia gave him a small, grateful smile before she leaned toward Thelma and took the older woman's trembling hands in her own. "It's Derek, Thelma," she began.

And as Daniel listened to the soft tones of Julia's voice as she told an elderly lady her husband of forty years had been shot dead for no obvious reason, he felt a shift deep inside his chest. Something had happened the moment he'd laid eyes on Julia Kershaw. Daniel found her completely and utterly infuriating but at the same time incredibly intelligent and fantastically sexy.

He knew there was much more going on with her than a desire for further advancement in her career. Certain rules would have to be adhered to if this investigation was going to proceed without mistakes. The mark on her arm and her obvious determination to be on that ship didn't fit with her concerned, sensitive gaze as she looked at Thelma now, or the way her own tears fell in silent harmony with that of a newly bereaved woman.

As his heart swelled a little more, Daniel Conway knew he wanted to get to the bottom of Julia Kershaw's secrets as much as he did this case.

****

Julia rocked Thelma back and forth in her arms like she would a troubled child. The older woman's sobs filled the room with such sorrow and desolation, Julia could do nothing but hold her tight in her arms while praying for the strength to help her. "It's going to be all right, it's going to be all right," she whispered.

She repeated the words like a mantra, hoping they'd do something to soothe Thelma's pain but knew at this moment, there was nothing she could say or do to make it any better. Eventually, Thelma's sobs subsided to quiet whimpering. Julia looked over her head at Daniel.

His head was respectfully lowered, his hands clasped tightly together so the knuckles showed white.

"Daniel?"

He lifted his head. "Yes?"

"Do you want to tell Thelma what happens next?" she asked, quietly. "What you're going to do to find Derek's killer?"

He cleared his throat. "Of course."

But before he could say more, Thelma shifted in Julia's arms and sat up straight. When she looked at Daniel, her soft dove-grey eyes were filled with pain and confusion.

"I knew he would end up dead. I told him so. I told him that he'd get killed or kill himself. One of the two."

Julia looked in shock from Thelma to Daniel, his eyes alert as he watched Thelma carefully. He leaned closer toward her, his elbows resting on his knees as he tried to keep his professional interest discreet, but Julia could tell by the sudden tightness in his jaw that whatever he had been thinking about a few moments before was forgotten.

She had seen a fleeting glimpse of the man inside when he had been silently sitting beside her, his frown telling her it was possible he was capable of some amount of compassion. But now that man was gone. Now he was a cop. A cop who needed answers and needed them fast.

She stood and took a seat on the arm of Thelma's chair, gently brushed the hair from Thelma's eyes. "What do you mean? Was Derek in trouble?"

"Trouble? Huh! That's an understatement." Thelma balled the handkerchief she held in her hand. Her voice broke. "The man was a fool!"

"Why, Thelma? You must tell Inspector Conway

anything that was going on with Derek when he was killed," urged Julia. "He's here to help."

Thelma slowly turned to face Daniel as though seeing him for the first time. "Inspector? Are you the one they've put in charge after Ed retired?"

"Yes, Thelma. I am."

"Oh, what I wouldn't give to have Ed here now. He'd know what to do." She turned to Julia. "When Phil was killed—"

Julia's stomach twisted and a bitter taste rose in her mouth. *Ssshh, Thelma. Don't do this. I don't want him to realize who I am. It's only a matter of time before he knows. Then he'll start treating me with kid gloves the same as everyone else.*

She leaned her face closer to Thelma's, willing her not to say any more. "What sort of trouble was Derek in, Thelma?" she asked.

But Daniel was standing and moving around the table toward her. She swallowed. He didn't speak to Julia or even look at her, instead he dropped to his haunches in front of Thelma. Julia slowly released her held breath. He obviously wasn't going to say anything right now, but he must have heard.

"Thelma?" he asked.

She wasn't listening. She was staring at the handkerchief in her hands, lost in thought with tears slowly trailing down her cheeks. Daniel touched a hand to hers.

"We're going to find whoever did this, I promise you."

"But you're so young and so new in town. Ed knew everyone in Corkley Park. Where will you start? How will you manage to find out who did this if you don't know anyone?"

Daniel smiled softly. "Inspector Langton may be retired but I have no shame in calling him if I think it necessary. He warned me Corkley Park was a town where everyone knew everyone else and I might need his help from time to time."

"He did?"

Daniel nodded. "Yep."

Julia's stomach turned all the way over as she saw the wobbly smile form at Thelma's lips. He'd made her smile, if only for a second, he'd made Thelma smile. Despite her reservations about him, Julia had to admit the man could be more sensitive than most. Credit where credit was due—so he could be nice.

It didn't mean he was any better than most cops.

"But before I can do anything else, Thelma," he was saying, "I need you to tell me what type of man Derek was? Who were his friends? What were his hobbies? Anything at all. Do you think you're up to that?"

Thelma studied his face for a long moment before a wistfulness settled over her features. "You're a very handsome man, Inspector. Do you know that? You remind me of my Derek at your age. He had the same jet black hair and devilish dark brown eyes." She let out a little laugh. "And I bet you're a hit with the ladies like he was too, aren't you?"

Julia bit back her own laugh as she saw, with perverted pleasure, the big, six foot two Inspector blush to the roots of his hair. Daniel opened his mouth to respond but nothing came out. Julia took his sudden inability to speak as her cue to cut in.

"Why don't you spare the poor Inspector any more blushes, Thelma and tell me what you meant about Derek. Was he in trouble?"

When Thelma turned back to Julia, her eyes were glassy

with tears. Despite her attempt at levity, Julia could see the woman who had been like a grandmother to her was barely holding it together.

"Oh, Thelma," she said, stealing an arm around

27

Thelma's shoulders. "Everything's going to be OK. Derek will always be here for you."

Thelma shook her head. "This is all his own fault. He brought this all on himself."

"What is? His murder? Don't try and get through this on your own, Thelma. You've got to tell us what you know."

"He was a silly man. A foolish man. A man with a head full of fantasy, a heart full of pride and a soul that would never believe all is not right in the world." She turned from Julia to Daniel. "My husband was in serious trouble, Inspector. He was a gambler, you see, and unfortunately he left it too late for me to do anything about the ludicrous amount of debt he had landed us both in."

Shock rushed through Julia's body. *Derek was a gambler?* She said nothing as Daniel leaned in closer to Thelma. "Derek was in debt?"

Thelma nodded. "Not just Derek, me too. Our money has always been thrown together. But he continued to lie to me. Use money that was mine as well as his to back horses, fund cards. Oh, the list goes on."

"And what about the boat?" Daniel pressed.

Her forehead creased in confusion. "I don't understand. The boat?"

Julia cleared her throat. "Derek was shot on board a boat, Thelma."

Thelma's eyes widened. "But Derek doesn't know anyone who owns a boat," she exclaimed. "Why would he be on a boat?"

"That's what we need to figure out, Mrs. Palmer," Daniel said. "Did he have business associates who he might have arranged to meet there? Or did anyone own a boat who came into the store, maybe?"

She slowly shook her head. "Was it a fishing boat? Derek liked to go out on the water and fish but

28

it's been months since he's even had any interest in doing that."

Daniel looked at Julia. "Could it have been a fishing boat? You said it was more like a yacht, didn't you?"

"It wasn't a yacht as such, but it was definitely designed with pleasure in mind rather than work." She took Thelma's hand. "Maybe Derek knew a relation who had a boat?"

She quickly shook her head, her voice rising, "There's nobody. Oh, whatever had he gotten himself into? I loved him so much, the silly man."

Julia's heart broke for the woman in front of her. "Oh, Thelma, I had no idea things were so bad."

Thelma gave a derisive laugh through her tears. "Things were so bad he'd started laundering money through the store for some loan sharks as interest payments." She dropped her head into her hands. "I'm so ashamed to be telling you this. But now he's dead, what's the use in keeping up appearances? The whole sorry mess of our lives will be the talk of the town before long."

Daniel lifted himself from the floor and sat on the settee again. "The press will not be informed of any details about Derek's gambling, Thelma. That information may turn out to be imperative to the case and so will be kept solely to the investigating team's knowledge. It is of no public interest. People will only know if you choose to tell them. You have my word."

She gave a grateful nod. "I don't know that there's anything else I can tell you."

Daniel shut his notebook and pushed it into his jacket pocket. "Why don't we leave it there for now and I'll come back in the morning?"

She dabbed at her eyes. "Thank you, Inspector."

It was nearing eight o'clock by the time Julia and Daniel left Thelma in the capable hands of her next door neighbor. They got into the car and pulled away in silence. Twilight was drawing in, turning the few wispy clouds above them salmon-pink. As they drove along the street, the imminent darkness reminded Julia how late it actually was.

"Oh, my God, I completely forgot! I'm supposed to be at the club working by eight o'clock tonight."

"Julia, you can't be serious. There's no way you can work tonight. You've had a massive shock and although you're still standing right now, don't think for one minute you won't fall. You need to go home and rest."

"I can't, you're going to have to drop me at the club."

"What club?"

"The Ship's Mate. I sing there and I'm supposed to be on stage in fifteen minutes."

"You sing? Is that what you'll be doing on the Princess II?"

"Uh-huh. A cool, clean, money-earning way out."

"Way out? From Corkley Park?"

Julia swallowed. "Whatever. Can you take me to the club or not?"

"But you shouldn't be working."

"Point taken, Inspector, but I still want to go."

He shook his head. "You're one stubborn woman, do you know that?"

She shrugged. "Yep."

The corners of his mouth twitched. "And I'm quickly learning there's no reasoning with you."

Julia bit back a response. As long as he got her to the club, she didn't care what he thought of her. As they drove down the promenade, Julia felt envious of the families and couples walking along the sea-front, laughing and having fun. They had no idea just how cruel and violent this world could be— or did they? Who really knew anyone? Thelma had never had any idea Derek was leading a double life until recently. Even Julia herself would never have thought a handful of dates with a guy would lead to him having such a deep, unhealthy interest in her. She rubbed at the bruise Marcus had left when he'd tried to make her understand the nonsense that had spewed from his mouth a few days earlier.

Who knew what secrets people had? Look what secrets she was hiding, herself.

She glanced across at Daniel and an unexpected sensation skittered across her skin. There was something quietly masculine about Daniel Conway. He carried himself with a subtle assurance, his eyes clear and focused as though he were always looking into the heart of the person he was speaking to.

Then again, maybe nothing and no one was what they seemed. Maybe it wasn't genuine concern in his brooding eyes at all, but perpetual suspicion.

Julia shivered involuntarily. Whatever it was, she could not ignore the tell-tale signals of attraction. He wore a short-sleeve shirt and she inhaled a deep breath as she watched the muscles in his arms flex and relax with each movement of the steering wheel. His strong profile and dark hair were nothing short of gorgeous.

Suddenly he turned. Heat surged to her cheeks.

He smiled. "You okay?"

"Uh-huh." She quickly looked out the window.

"Are you sure?"

"I'm fine."

There was a pause before he spoke again.

"I still can't convince you to go home instead of this club?"

She turned back to face him. "Nope. Even if I wasn't singing tonight, I'd still want to tell Jacob about Derek before he finds out from someone else."

"Jacob?"

"My boss. He and Derek have been friends since they were teenagers. Anyway, I *need* to sing right

31

now. Singing helps me relieve stress."

"Fair enough. I find a bottle of wine and a good meal at Simone's does it for me."

She grinned. "So you've fallen victim to the delights of Simone's apple crumble already, then?"

"Can't you tell?" he asked, patting a non-existent stomach.

She looked down and let her eyes linger longer than necessary at his groin area. When she looked back up, he lifted a questioning eyebrow before turning back to the road.

Julia cleared her throat before flicking an imaginary piece of lint from her shorts. "Yes, well. I'll stick with the singing. Her apple crumble has a habit of going sticking at my hips."

"From what I've seen of your hips, you've got nothing to worry about."

She snapped her head around to look at him. "I'm sorry?"

The fading light did not hide the burst of color from the collar of his shirt to the whole of his face. "I shouldn't have said that...ignore me, I'm...sorry."

But instead of feeling affronted, Julia hid her thrilled grin by turning back to look out the window.

Chapter Three

Daniel followed Julia through the darkened main room of The Ship's Mate, toward the bar. Decorated like the interior of an ancient pirate ship, the dark brown planks of the walls teemed with nets, lethal looking cutlasses and replica pistols. Parrots and beer jugs were scattered around the place, and a huge Jolly Roger flag swathed the entire ceiling from corner to corner.

Boisterous laughter and squeals of delight filtered above the rock music blasting out of the camouflaged speakers. Each member of the bar staff, the band on the stage, and the waitresses wore full pirate costume. Daniel smiled. It had been a long time since he'd let go and had a good night out like the people around him were now. Maybe when this case was finished, he would remedy that.

That thought drew his attention to the back of the toned legs and denim-encased backside ahead of him. There was something about Julia Kershaw's constant challenge of everything he said, and her obvious distrust in him, that made her impossibly intriguing. And wonderfully attractive.

They finally shouldered their way to the bar and Julia jumped up onto one of the vacant stools.

"Hey, Jacob, over here!" she yelled above the boom-boom of the Bon Jovi's 'You Give Love a Bad Name.'

A man in his late fifties slowly strolled toward her. Dressed as a ship's captain, Daniel guessed the eye patch and blackened teeth were supposed to be intimidating, but the mischief glinting in his one blue eye completely undermined the intention. Jacob came to a stop in front of them and adjusted the brim of his three-pointed hat.

"Ah-ha! She finally decides to grace us with her presence. Half an hour late for the start of her set but who cares?"

Julia waved a dismissive hand. "Don't start. Believe me, I've got good reason. But before I say anything, I need a drink."

"Is that so?" He fisted his hands on his hips. "And tell me, fair lady, why I should honor your request?"

"Because if you don't I won't sing tonight and you'll have a riot on your hands."

Jacob huffed. "You think this lot would even notice? You're not that special, you know."

"Why, you—"

Jacob leaned across the bar and snatched her into a hug. "I'm just glad you're here and safe. You're never late."

Daniel smiled as he watched the exchange. It appeared Julia was loved wherever she went. And as she turned her laughing green eyes to his, Daniel felt that hit himself.

"Inspector Conway," Julia held out a hand toward Jacob. "Let me introduce you to Jacob Kent. My boss, who also likes to think he has a say in my personal life." She smiled. "Jacob? This is Corkley Park's new Detective Inspector. Daniel Conway."

Jacob's eyebrows shot to the brim of his hat.

"Detective Inspector?" He looked from Daniel back to Julia, his eyes wide. "Never thought I'd see the day when you'd let a cop within ten yards of you let alone *that* close."

Daniel discreetly stepped back from where he'd edged in beside Julia. "So you've noticed her aversion to cops too," he said, smiling. "Want to tell me about it?"

"Don't take any notice of him, Inspector. Jacob hasn't got a clue about anything," snapped Julia, glaring at her boss.

"Haven't got a clue she says," Jacob laughed. "Is that so? Well to my mind that damn bank manager must still be giving you hassle, otherwise why the hell would you be strolling in here with a cop?" He cracked open a bottle of beer and put it on the bar in front of her. "What have I told you, Julia? You don't need to involve anybody else in your business, just let me deal with him."

In the semi-darkness of the room, Daniel watched Julia's face pale. The smooth skin of her neck shifted as she swallowed and the hands that reached for the beer bottle trembled ever so slightly.

"The reason DI Conway is here has nothing to do with Marcus. For God's sake, will you stop and think before you start shouting all sorts of things around this bar?" she asked, through clenched teeth. "He's here about something serious, not a pain in the ass like Marcus."

Daniel placed a hand on the bar and looked from Julia to Jacob and back again. "One of you want to tell me what's going on? Who's Marcus? And what has he done to you that your boss here thinks warrants police protection?" he asked, meeting her furious gaze.

Jacob leaned forward. "Marcus Lowell is a son of a bitch—"

"Jacob! For crying out loud," Julia protested.

Daniel leaned an elbow on the bar. "Well?"

He watched her struggle, saw the battle she was having with herself deep inside. She picked up her beer, took a gulp and then shrugged. "He's some guy I had five or six dates with that's all. It's nothing. It's over."

Daniel noted Jacob's grunt of disapproval but kept his eyes locked on Julia's. "And is it over to him as well?"

Her gaze never wavered. "Yes."

"He doesn't want there to be a seventh date?"

"No."

He knew she was lying, but there wasn't much he could do about it until he got back to the station and looked up Marcus Lowell's name in the database. Along with Julia's, of course. After a long moment, he broke eye contact and turned to Jacob. "Is there somewhere we can go to talk more privately, Mr. Kent?"

"What do we need to talk about that can't be said right here?"

Julia crossed her arms. "Don't waste your breath, Inspector. You can see what an obnoxious, bull-headed idiot he can be at times..."

"Don't you talk to me like that," said Jacob. "I'm like a second father to you."

"There's something I need to tell you, Jacob. Why don't you shut up and listen for once in your life?"

Julia and Jacob locked eyes for a long moment before the fight left her and her shoulders dropped, along with her voice. "Oh, God, Jacob, how do I tell you this?"

The argument forgotten, Daniel watched Jacob slide his hand across the bar and take Julia's fingers. "Hey, what's up, sweetheart? What's the matter?"

"Jacob—" she began. "I need to speak to you about something before I get changed. It's about Derek."

"Derek? Well, why didn't you say?" He laughed. "What's that idiot been up to now?"

"He's dead, Jacob. Murdered."

For a long moment, he said nothing. He stared at Julia, his head tilted to the side, the expression on his face like that of a bewildered child. He reached for a bottle behind him, filled the glass with scotch and knocked half of it back in one go. Daniel could only describe the expression in his eyes as blank when he looked at her.

"And how is it you know about this before the rest of us?" he asked. "I always thought this place was the slipstream for town news."

"I knew because I saw it happen."

He coughed. "You were there? Jesus, Julia!"

"I know, I know."

"Are you OK?"

"Physically, yes. Mentally? Ask me again in a few days."

"Shit."

Jacob looked into the amber depths of his glass before lifting it to his lips and draining it. He wiped a hand across his mouth. "Well, I'm sorry you had to see it, but I'm not sorry he's dead."

"Jacob!" Julia cried. "What are you talking about? You were friends."

He laughed derisively. "Friends? Derek Palmer stopped being any friend of mine a long time ago."

Daniel pursed his lips shut. He carefully watched Julia freeze for a second before turning to face him. She looked scared. "I don't understand why he's saying that any more than you do."

Daniel looked expectantly at Jacob. "Well?"

Jacob pulled himself up straight. "Well, what?"

"It seems to me, Mr. Kent, that Julia was expecting at least a modicum of upset from you but from where I'm standing the news isn't all that unwelcome. Am I right?"

Jacob sniffed. "Yes, that's right."

Julia snatched her handbag from the top of the bar. "Do you need me to stay here, Inspector?"

Daniel shook his head. "I think I can take it from here."

"I'll leave you to it then. Oh, and for the record,

Jacob. I'm finding it incredibly hard to look at you right now."

"Well, why don't you just get changed and step up on that stage and do what you're paid to do?"

Daniel felt like he was watching a father and daughter fight. Despite the current level of tension buzzing around them right now, he felt the beginnings of a smile. But it instantly dissolved when Julia suddenly turned her scowl on him.

"And am I right in assuming you'll be staying here even longer now?" she demanded.

"I'm going to ask Jacob a few more questions, if that's all right with you," he said.

"It's not as though I can argue with a cop, is it?"

His mouth twitched as he met her angry glare. "No, I suppose not."

She waved a hand in the air. "Oh, do whatever you want." She paused. "And for God's sake stop laughing at me."

"I'm not laughing..."

But she'd already walked away and was disappearing up a spiral staircase at the back of the club. Shaking his head, Daniel slid onto her vacated bar stool and leaned an elbow on the bar.

"She certainly says what she's thinking, doesn't she?" he asked, finally managing to drag his eyes away from her backside.

"She's a good girl, my Julia."

"I can see how fond you are of each other."

Kent watched him carefully. "Like I said, she's a good girl. A damn good girl who deserves some happiness."

Daniel arched an eyebrow. "She's not happy, then?"

"Not with that damn waste of space..." He stopped. "Did you come in here with her to tell me about Derek being killed? Or is there another reason you're with her?"

"What do you mean?"

"Is she under police protection after seeing Derek bumped off, is that why you're with her?"

"Bumped off? That's a pretty callous way to sum up a friend's murder."

"Yeah, well, like I said, he hasn't been my friend for a while now."

Daniel met his gaze and felt the hairs on the back of his neck rise. Kent's eyes were cold, steely and something else...dangerous.

"And why is that?" he asked, carefully.

"I don't like anyone who lies, cheats and breaks promises with no explanation, Inspector. That don't make me wrong, it makes me right."

Daniel held his stare. "Did you know Derek was in trouble?"

"Tough. We all got our problems. Derek Palmer had deals to see through and he never did."

"Did he have a deal with you?"

Kent whipped the towel from his shoulder and slapped it back and forth across the bar. "He owed me money. A lot of money I never saw again. Yes, he lied to me and yes, I was pissed off."

Daniel studied him. He wasn't the killer, because Julia would have recognized him, but that didn't mean he couldn't be involved. He took a deep breath. "Fair enough."

"That's it?" Kent asked. "You're not going to haul my ass to the station for questioning?"

"Should I?"

"No, but most cops don't care whether or not they should do a lot of things."

"Ah, so it's not just Julia, then?"

"What?"

"It's not just Julia who hates cops in this town."

"She's got good reason, don't you think? As far as I'm concerned, you lot have been a pain in my side ever since I swiped my first push bike from Ma

Mclean's front yard."

"So that's your reason. What's Julia's?"

Kent narrowed his eyes and Daniel knew he'd just asked the worst question possible. "If you seriously don't know, *Inspector,* I suggest you find out, and pretty damn quick, because Julia won't be the one to tell you."

"I'm not most cops, you know, Jacob," he said.

"I'm sure we'll find out in time."

His tone was icy cold and Daniel thought it best to let the subject drop. He had every intention of taking Kent's advice and do his own investigating once he left here. But first he was curious to hear Julia sing. He licked dry lips.

"How about you pass me one of those beers?" he said, pointing to the fridges behind the bar.

Kent pushed himself away from the bar and grabbed a bottle.

"Enjoy," he said, and slammed it down on the bar.

Before Daniel could respond, the lights of the bar changed from red, to gold, to a soft amber yellow. The stage was plunged into darkness. Daniel picked up his beer and swiveled around on his seat to watch the show as several silhouetted figures strolled onto the stage and took up their instruments.

After a few tense seconds and a lingering drum roll, the stage exploded into light and the crowd erupted.

"Ladies and gentleman, apologies for the delay, here she is...our favorite girl...Julia!"

She ran onto the stage and Daniel froze, his beer bottle at his lips. She wore thigh-length pirate boots, a short black skirt and a frilly white blouse with the buttons left open just enough to reveal the smooth curve of her breasts. She looked so damn hot, the heat was almost unbearable.

But it was Julia, not the costume, that caused

Daniel to guzzle his beer like a man dying of thirst.

Not only did she look achingly beautiful, but her voice transformed the song she was singing into the sexiest, most erotic serenade he'd ever had to resist. She pulled at the heartstrings of the audience with a soft, seductive ballad, her voice husky and deep, warm and full. It swept over his nerve endings, causing the hairs at the back of his neck to stand to attention. He swallowed down the last of his beer and wiped a hand across his mouth. He felt a knock on his elbow.

"Want another one?" Kent laughed. "Looks like you need it."

Daniel shook his empty bottle and licked his dry lips.

"Can't. I'm driving."

"Poor you. The way your tongue's hanging out looking at my Julia, you may die of dehydration before she finishes her set."

Daniel cursed as Jacob walked away chuckling to himself. He had a murder to solve and the woman who was making his pants suddenly feel incredibly tight was the only the link he had.

****

The next morning Julia awoke to bright sunlight filtering through her soft plum curtains. She stretched languorously before reaching out an arm toward the bedside clock—just past eleven. She dropped back against the pillows and let the night before play through her mind. Daniel had disappeared before her half-way break, leaving a message with Jacob that he'd been called out and would catch up with her in the morning.

Jacob had told her he'd had the distinct impression something else had driven him away but he wouldn't say what. But it turned out for the best because Marcus had stumbled into the club at midnight, stinking drunk and once again, proclaiming his undying love for her. She shuddered. That love had soon turned to something much more unnerving when Julia had explained for the fiftieth time in the last two months there was nothing between them and never would be.

Fortunately, he had left without any fuss this time. The last thing she needed was another physical struggle with him when she was likely to be in Daniel's company for the next few days. Not that Marcus would be stupid enough to touch her in public. She looked at the fading bruise on her wrist. Marcus had apologized for grabbing her, but Julia knew she still had to be on her guard with him. He was getting more and more unpredictable and she just hoped he didn't find out about her impending departure. It could be the thing that pushed his adoration over the edge into obsession.

She exhaled a slow breath as her mind filled with Daniel's face. It was no use denying the attraction she felt for him and it didn't matter that he appeared kind and patient—the complete opposite of Marcus. Daniel was a cop. If her mother could've seen into Julia's dreams last night, she would have never spoken to her again.

She covered her face with her hands. She had to focus. The only people who knew she was leaving were her parents, her friend Suzie, Jacob, and now Daniel. If Marcus found out, she was terrified he would try to stop her. She dropped her hands. Intellectually, she knew if Marcus carried on the way he was, the next step would be to call in the cops—

But how could she? How could she trust a cop after one of them had taken her brother's life?

She swallowed hard, threw back the bedcovers and marched into the en-suite bathroom. A long, hot bath was the first thing on her agenda. Then she would go to the police station to see if there was any progress with the investigation. She turned on the taps, added a long stream of scented bubble bath, and waited for the tub to fill.

Ten minutes later, she slipped beneath the bubbles and thought of Jacob. After she'd gotten rid of Marcus, Jacob had been adamant that he take her home in case Marcus was still hanging around outside the club, or worse, her house. Jacob's reaction to Derek's death had not been what she'd expected. Even when they were alone, he hadn't asked one question about what she seen at the beach. It made her sad to think such a strong friendship could be reduced to that level of resentment.

She'd asked Jacob what had happened between him and Derek but Jacob had refused to tell her. She could only assume that deep-down, Jacob was truly hurting. The open anger on his face had convinced her that whatever had occurred had been serious. Jacob was not one to hold a grudge, but Julia could tell by the way his fists had clenched and unclenched on the steering wheel last night, he had meant it when he'd said he felt nothing that Derek was dead.

"One way or another I'll find out, Jacob," she said aloud. "There's no way I'll let Derek's funeral pass without you saying a proper goodbye."

An hour later, she walked into her cottage-style kitchen, and opened the refrigerator. She took out orange juice, eggs and milk, and decided to make herself a breakfast cum lunch before she headed into town. She didn't want Daniel to have to come looking for her and turn up at her house.

She closed the refrigerator door and that was when she saw the note taped to the outside of the window. Everything slipped from her hands to the tiled floor with a crash. Her breathing became harried as she attempted to stem the sharp thudding in her chest.

"My God, he's lost his mind," she whispered.

Nausea rose in her throat and her hands began to shake.

WHO'S THE COP, JULIA? DON'T DO ANYTHING STUPID, MY LOVE.

She rushed outside and ripped the note from the window before going back into the kitchen and locking the door behind her. Her body trembled as she slid to the floor. Why was Marcus doing this?

Six dates. Six dates and the man had turned into an obsessive, out-of-control lunatic. Who was to say what he would do next? She dropped her head into her hands and tried to steady her breathing. She had nine days before the Princess II left town and in that time anything could happen.

Maybe I should tell Daniel?

No, she didn't need or want a cop's involvement. She would keep Marcus at arm's length, not do anything to provoke his anger and when the ship left, she'd quietly slip away without looking back. Marcus was a successful and respected bank manager, his fixation with her was only a passing phase. It had to be.

She heard a tap, tap, tap at the window and snapped her head up, expecting it to be Marcus. But it wasn't. It was Daniel.

"Great, that's all I need right now." She heaved herself up from the floor and swiped the tears from her cheeks before she opened the door. "Isn't it usual for visitors to knock at the front door?" she asked.

His smile was easy—wonderful—and completely disarming.

"Apparently not in this town. Thelma gave me your address and told me to come round the back. I quote, 'Julia isn't one for formality, just let yourself in'. At least I didn't do that."

"She's right about the formality. Think yourself lucky I'm not in my pajamas."

"That would've been fine with me."

She narrowed her eyes. "Excuse me?"

He lifted his shoulders. "It would have been no worse than finding you sitting on your kitchen floor."

Heat flared in her cheeks. "I was contemplating the day ahead."

"Really? Sitting amongst broken eggs and orange juice?" he asked, arching an eyebrow.

She looked around. The floor was a mess. The orange juice had mixed with the eggs, forming a gooey substance that was going to be hell to wipe up. "Um...I had a bit of an accident. I don't like spiders and this huge one jumped out from behind the counter..."

"Julia?"

She met his gaze. "Yes?"

"Instead of trying to come up with a story neither of us is going to believe, why don't I agree not to ask any questions and you go upstairs and change? I'll clear up down here."

"Change? Why do I..." She looked down and froze. She hadn't even felt the juice spill on the front of her T-shirt, which now clung to her breasts, leaving Daniel with a pretty accurate idea of her cup size. "Oh."

She was not surprised to see that recurring amusement on his face again.

"Why don't you go on upstairs," he said. "I'll still be here when you come back down. We've got a lot to get through today."

"Right. Yes, yes, we do."

Still smiling, he reached for a cloth, dropped to his knees and began wiping the floor. She may have felt like a complete idiot but that didn't make her blind. She gave a small smile of her own to see how perfect his ass and thighs looked encased in faded denim, bending over her kitchen floor. He looked up and caught her staring.

"Everything OK?"

Her cheeks burned hot. "Um, sure, OK, right then. I'll...um...yes."

He turned back to the floor and Julia used the opportunity to snatch Marcus' note from the trash bin before fleeing for the stairs.

She closed her bedroom door behind her and flung open the wardrobe. Quickly stripping off her clothes, she threw them in the laundry basket, washed her soaked chest, then pulled on a dress and ballet pumps. Daniel must think her a complete moron. The first time she'd met him, she barged into his office like a maniac, then he'd accompanied her to the club and seen her in her full pirate regalia. Today, he dropped by her house to find her sitting on the kitchen floor wearing half a pint of orange juice on her shirt.

Clearly the man had no other leads to go on regarding Derek's murder or he wouldn't be relying on her as a witness. She grabbed a hair band, quickly brushed her hair into a ponytail, and glanced toward the window. Unease prickled the hairs at the nape of her neck. Marcus must have been watching her yesterday before he came to the club. How else would he have known about the time she had spent with Daniel?

His reputation in Corkley Park was high class and there was no chance Marcus would risk losing his job. He was an intelligent man and would soon come to his senses. Julia knew she could look after herself and in just nine days, she would be away from here. There was no need to involve the cops. No need at all.

With her mind made up, she headed back downstairs and into the kitchen.

"Wow, you aren't too bad at this cleaning business, are you?" she said, looking at the spotless floor. "Well—for a guy."

He executed a bow. "Thank you, ma'am. I must say, that dress looks a lot better than the T-shirt did."

She smiled and pointed a finger at him. "Not a word. You say anything to the guys down at the station, I'll never forgive you."

He raised his hands in mock surrender. "I promise. Lips sealed."

Their eyes locked and Julia felt something as warm and as comforting as cashmere envelop her. She cleared her throat. "So...where to first?"

His gaze didn't move.

"Daniel?"

He blinked and the moment dissolved. "Yes, the case." He pulled out a chair at the kitchen table. "Could we sit down for a minute?"

"Sure." She had a horrible feeling he was going to say something she didn't want to hear. She tentatively sat down.

"Is something wrong?" she asked.

He sat opposite her at the table. "I looked up Marcus Lowell's name on the database late last night," he said. "He has no record."

Damn Jacob and his big mouth. She swallowed and forced a smile. "Of course he hasn't. You shouldn't take any notice of Jacob. He's overprotective and has a vivid imagination. No one will ever be good enough for me as far as he's concerned."

"And Lowell is an ex-boyfriend, yes?"

"Yes, and ex is the key word here."

"And he's not harassing you?"

"No."

He stared at her for a long moment and Julia's heartbeat thumped steadily in her ears but she managed to keep her eyes level with his. "He is a bank manager, for crying out loud. He's a respected guy in town. His attention will fizzle out soon

47

enough, trust me. It happens to singers all the time."

He studied her. "Are you sure about that?"

"Yes."

"But you'll let me know if it gets to the stage when you feel uncomfortable?"

She laughed, lifted a hand to her head in a salute. "Absolutely, Inspector."

He opened his mouth to say something else but then closed it again. At last, he stood. "Good. Well, shall we get going?"

She exhaled. "Sure."

"We'll go straight back to the station and have a look at a few mug shots to begin with," Daniel said, still carefully watching her. "I know you said you couldn't see the killer properly but something might nudge a memory. It's worth a try."

She pulled her bag from the counter. "Ready when you are."

"I'd suggest sharing my car but I know I'm going to be tied up all day and won't be able to give you a lift back later."

"No problem, I'll follow behind you," Julia said, grabbing her keys.

They drove back to the station and Julia walked through the open plan office toward Daniel's private office. Several police men and women milled about, their faces tense with concentration.

Their presence caused Julia to shiver involuntarily. Corkley Park had always been a quiet town that got by on a Detective Inspector, his sergeant and one or two foot police. At least ten other officers had been brought over from the neighboring town—a cold-blooded killer was still out there, could even have left the country by now.

"Are you OK?" Daniel's fingers touched her elbow.

She blew out a breath. "I see you've drafted in extra troops."

Daniel tapped his fingers across a ring binder sitting on his desk. "Needs must. We have to get on top of this, each hour that goes by is another hour Derek's killer could be getting further away." He rubbed a hand along his jaw and sat down in the leather chair behind his desk. "I won't lie to you, Julia. The first twenty-four hours are the most important in any investigation. Here, take a seat."

She sat down and he pushed the binder toward her. "Have a look through these and let me know if any of them seems familiar. Take your time. Go over them again and again until you're positive there is no chance it could have been any of them who shot Derek."

Julia opened the binder to page after page of pictures. "I don't know that this will do any good. I didn't get a proper look at him at all. He had his face turned in the opposite direction most of the time."

Daniel reached forward. "Just try."

Her eyes dropped to his hand, which now lay covering hers and a jolt shot through her stomach. He was making her feel things she had no business feeling. She was here to help find Derek's killer, yet her body was completely betraying every virtuous intention. Slowly she slipped her hand from under his and turned the first page over. "You'd better leave me to it."

"I'll be right outside if you need me."

He left the door open and Julia watched him walk into the main arena of activity. His encouraging smile of just a few seconds ago had disappeared as he raised his voice over the chattering in the room to get his team's attention. Silence descended instantaneously. He stood at his full six feet two inches, his feet apart and hands fisted at his hips.

Demanding a thorough investigation and intelligent policing, he fired one question after another at each member of his staff. He spoke with calm authority, but when a voice at the back of the room made an inappropriate quip, he slammed his hand down so hard on a nearby desk that Julia jumped in her seat.

He might treat her with kindness and consideration, but Julia was witnessing first hand that Daniel Conway was also a man who wanted results. There was every possibility he would get them. And from what little she was learning about him, it was getting harder and harder to keep believing that those results would only be achieved by his use of brute force or unnecessary violence.

If she changed her view of the police because of Daniel, she'd be carrying out the ultimate betrayal to her brother's memory. She could never allow that to happen. Her mother had lost one child, she didn't deserve to be estranged from another.

Blinking back the burning tears in her eyes, Julia turned her attention to the mug shots. She looked at each in turn, hoping something would flick a switch in her memory and she would be able to pinpoint Derek's killer.

An hour later, she closed the binder feeling dejected. She was circling her fingers at her temples when Daniel came back through the open door.

"Nothing. Absolutely nothing," she said.

He tossed some papers down onto the desk. "Don't beat yourself up about it. It was a long shot. We're pursuing other avenues."

"I thought you had nothing to go on."

"Sure, we do."

"There's no need to lie to me, Inspector."

His eyes met hers. "I thought we'd progressed from Inspector to Daniel." He smiled. "Well, at least when we're alone."

She met his smile. "There's no need to make me feel better, *Daniel*. I know we'll find out whoever did this to Derek."

"Good. Because we have other leads. Good leads."

"But I'm your sole witness. No one else saw Derek killed," Julia insisted. "What other leads could you possibly have?"

He held up a hand and began counting off each finger. "Number one, murder always starts with the victim, not the killer. Number two, we find the boat, we find the killer. Number three, Derek was a gambler."

Julia creased her brow. "I don't understand."

"Gambling is an addiction. Gamblers mix with other gamblers." He walked up and down in front of her, his handsome face set. "I've got the team working on the first two points, we're going to take the third."

"There's that we again."

He spun around to face her. "I want you to come with me to the betting office. Everyone in town seems to know and like you. It will make my job a lot easier if I don't have to battle through a mile high wall of distrust everywhere I go."

"But aren't I included in that in that circle of mistrust?"

He smiled. "I think yours is down to half a mile now at least."

She grinned. "You think so, do you?"

"Yep." He snatched up a bunch of keys from the desk. "You coming?"

She plucked her bag from the back of the chair. "Right behind you. Oh, and the good news is my friend Suzie works there, and I can say without a doubt she'll be able to get someone to open up a bit down there."

"Great. An inside ally is always a bonus."

Chapter Four

Daniel pulled up at the kerb outside the betting
shop. He had been delayed for a few minutes back at
the station, so Julia had gone on ahead without him.
But even when he'd maneuvered his car so close to
hers they were practically bumper to bumper, she
didn't notice. Her cell phone was pressed to her ear
as her hands gestured frantically. Whoever she was
talking to was peeving her off big time.

He continued to watch her and thought back to
what else he had found out last night and not had
the guts to tell her this morning. When she'd first
said her name yesterday, the link between her and
the accidental death of twenty-one-year-old Philip
Kershaw had not crossed his mind. But now the
grim reality was he was sitting there, watching the
sister of a young man shot down in the prime of his
life by a cop.

Her blatant distrust of him was completely
valid. Her obvious distaste at just having to look at
him was understandably justified. But with the
knowledge he now had, all he wanted to do was
convince her to trust the police again—better yet,
make her trust *him*.

He knew he should have come clean this
morning about her brother's death, but when he'd
seen her sitting in the orange juice, he couldn't do it.
Something had stopped him. Something so
unprofessional, if it was to ever to seep from inside
his mind and out into the open, it could get him
demoted, or worse, struck off.

All he'd wanted to do was break the door down

and go to her. Her knees had been cradled to her chest like a frightened child. Even though with a blink of her big, green eyes the flash of terror had vanished, he'd clearly seen it when she'd looked to his tap at the window. He wanted Julia Kershaw to trust him enough to tell him herself what was happening to make her that afraid.

Daniel wanted her to like him enough to tell him about her brother, herself, too.

He took a deep breath. Was he playing a dangerous game? Possibly. But he was willing to take that risk in order to make her understand all cops weren't bad guys.

He slipped the keys from the ignition, got out of the car and stood on the steps to the betting shop, waiting for her. Eventually she snapped the phone shut and got out of the car. She slammed the door shut with a resounding thud.

"Everything all right?" he asked.

She jumped and snapped her head up to look at him. "Do you always stand around watching people having private conversations?" she demanded, her cheeks flushing a deep scarlet.

He raised his eyebrows. He had allowed himself to believe he might be softening her resolve a little but from her tone of her voice he was way off. "What's wrong?"

"Everything is fine. Are we going in?" she asked, nodding toward the open door of the betting shop.

"Why don't you wait a few minutes to cool off?" he asked, quietly watching her.

"What?"

"You look kind of fired up."

She crossed her arms. "Is that so?"

"Yep."

They stood facing each other and Daniel's stomach knotted, looking into her angry eyes. It was a sad thing to admit, but God, he found her sexy when she was mad.

"Don't even think about laughing at me again, Inspector." "Excuse me?"

"You're doing that thing with the corner of your mouth again."

He smiled. "What thing?"

The color of her cheeks darkened. "You know. That...that thing."

"Sorry," he said, taking a tiny step closer. "What thing?"

She stepped back and held her palms up like a shield. "Forget it. Look, I'm fine. Are we going in or not? I was planning to have something to eat and a shower before my set tonight."

"You're on edge, Julia," he said.

She laughed dryly. "You think that's unusual after what I went through yesterday?"

Without thinking, he gently cupped a hand to her chin.

She immediately stiffened.

"The conversation you were having just now was not about yesterday," he said.

"And how do you know?"

"I just do."

"Really?" She lifted a hand and swatted his fingers away. "Do you mind?"

"Sorry." He took a step back. "I shouldn't have done that."

"No, you shouldn't have."

"It isn't professional."

"It's not professional at all."

"But..." He swallowed. *I want to touch you.* "I'd like to help if I can," he finally said.

She hesitated, her eyes searching his for the briefest of seconds before she turned away and looked up the street. "Why don't you just tell me how you want to handle this once we go inside? I'm here to help you with the case. You have no right to ask me about anything else."

Her jaw was set when she met his eyes again, but the unshed tears confirmed Julia Kershaw was hurting. Daniel wanted to say so much more to her, but knew now was not the time to push it. "You're right. I'm sorry."

Her shoulders relaxed a little. "Apology accepted. So...what happens next?"

He glanced toward the betting shop. "I want to find out how Derek was getting the money to gamble. Thelma said once she'd found out about the gambling, she looked after all the money. She gave him nothing spare. I'm hoping one of his gambling buddies will be able to point me in the right direction."

"Don't be surprised if the customers aren't very generous with the information. People around here don't like snitching on each other."

"Fair enough, but I don't think they're the type of people who would want to stop me from finding the man who killed their local store owner, either."

She smiled softly. "You're right. They're not. They'll help, I'm sure of it."

He lifted his arm to the side, gesturing for her to go in ahead of him. She took a step forward and then stopped.

"Look, before we go in, I need to warn you about Suzie."

Daniel frowned. "What about her?"

"She's..." She paused, as though searching for the right words. "Do you know what?" she asked, waving a dismissive hand in front of her. "I'll let you find out for yourself."

Daniel shrugged and walked inside, leaving Julia to follow on behind.

Kendricks' Bookies was not the type of place Daniel would have chosen to take a woman of Julia's caliber. A brown and off-white curtain hung at the door and when he pushed it to the side, the smell of stale tobacco and fast food hit them full force. It appeared no one left Kendricks to even go eat. To the compulsive gambler it clearly made more sense to order in, rather than risk missing the next race.

They weaved their way through the punters, heading for the front desk. The cashier looked about forty, but was obviously determined to stay in her hey-day of the early 1980s. She stood behind a pane of protective glass, her light brown hair three times the size of her head, and sprayed to within an inch of its life. The shoulder pads of her shiny red blouse scraped the sides of the minuscule booth.

She looked up and flashed him a grin the size of Great Britain, before hitching her massive bosom onto the counter, allowing her terrifying cleavage to stretch against the deep V of her blouse. Daniel ignored Julia's snigger behind him.

"Good afternoon, I'm Detective Inspector Daniel Conway."

"Detective Inspector, yum, yum!" she said, giving a lewd wink.

He held out his ID. "And you are?"

"Suzie Parsons, but you can call me what the hell you like, sugar pie."

"Well, Ms. Parsons, we are here—"

"Looking to handcuff me and throw me over your shoulder and out of here, I hope." Suzie grinned.

Not wanting to encourage her, Daniel ignored the comment. "We're here to talk to a few of your customers in connection with an ongoing investigation."

"Aw, can we have a little fun first? Just you and me?"

Daniel glared at her. "No, Miss Parsons, we can't."

She tutted. "Spoilsport. Anyway, who's we? I can

only see you from where I'm sitting. Not that it isn't a mighty fine view, darlin'."

He stepped to the side. "I believe you know Miss Julia Kershaw, she'll be helping..."

"Hi, sweetie! How you doing?"

Julia smiled. "I'm fine, Suzie. I can see you've dressed appropriately for work, as usual."

"Why, thank you. You know I always try to look my best. Not that it's appreciated by any of the boys in here," she muttered. "I'm sure this lot wouldn't notice if I walked in with tassels on my nipples and glitter on my ass."

Daniel's insides gave a lurch just thinking about that particular vision, but Julia laughed out loud and pressed a hand to her belly. "You crack me up, Suze. A night out with you is just what I need right now."

Suzie's face broke into a tentative smile. "Sure, sweetie, name the time and place and I'll be there."

Daniel stepped forward. "Look, I hate to interrupt the organizing of your social life, ladies, but we're here on official police business."

The two women exchanged a look and Daniel rolled his eyes. Women. He drew his notebook from his pocket.

"Right, I'll get started then..."

Suzie held up her hands. "There's no need to get your knickers in a twist, Inspector. We all need to laugh, you know. Now, what's this investigation all about? You said you've got some questions? Well, there isn't a lot I don't know about the goings on in this place, I can tell you. I spend half my life in this God forsaken place."

Daniel put a hand on the counter and lowered his voice. "Yesterday a man was murdered..."

"Murdered! Who? Oh, my God!" Suzie clasped a ringed hand to her throat.

Julia stepped closer. "It's all right, Suze."

The color had drained from Suzie's face and her eyes were filled with terror as she looked from Julia back to Daniel.

"It...wasn't one of my guys, was it? Oh, please tell me it wasn't one of the stupid oafs who come in here day in, day out driving me up the wall."

The tears in her eyes and tremble in her bottom lip gave no substance to the words tumbling from her mouth. Daniel guessed it was far more likely that Suzie loved each and every one of her customers.

Julia reached forward and took Suzie's hand through the gap at the bottom of the protective glass. "It was Derek, Suzie. I'm so sorry."

Suzie swayed on her feet before dropping back onto the stool behind her. Tears drew lines of electric blue mascara down her cheeks. "Derek? Oh, my God."

"I was there when it happened."

"What?" her friend cried, her eyes wide. "You were *there*?"

"Yes, I saw him shot."

Suzie blanched. "You *saw* it?"

"I was at the beach and I noticed this boat. And then...and then. Oh, Suze, he threw him overboard like he was a piece of rubbish."

"Oh, honey."

"He was dressed all in black with this cap pulled down over his face, Suze. I can't tell the police a single thing about him. It's hopeless."

Suzie squeezed Julia's hand. "We'll find out who did this. We have to. Oh, poor, Thelma. I told the stupid man to tell her what was going on. He'd got himself into such a damn mess, trying to cover his tracks and keep her from knowing anything. Why do men think we need protecting all the damn time?"

Daniel's interest sparked. "You knew about Derek's debts?"

Her fingers smeared the zigzags across her cheekbones. "Uh-huh. He'd lost an awful lot of weight, at least thirty pounds, he was constantly wringing his hands. I knew something was wrong. These guys trust me to keep their secrets and I always do, but it doesn't stop me from encouraging them to tell their wives what's going on. Especially when you have a wife like Thelma. I knew she'd do everything she could to help him."

Julia sighed. "He did tell her, Suze, and she did try to help, but he was in deeper than even Thelma could manage."

Daniel leaned forward, lowering his voice. "Did Derek mention any dealings with loan sharks?"

"Loan sharks? Derek was involved with loan sharks?" Suzie's baby-blue eyes were wide. "Aw, the stupid, stupid man."

Daniel glanced around him. The clientele eyed him suspiciously through a haze of cigarette smoke. It seemed highly unlikely they'd answer his questions with particular candidness. Maybe they'd get a whole lot further if Suzie asked the questions. From what she'd just said, she held the customers' trust and they would certainly feel less threatened by her than by the new Detective Inspector.

"Would you be willing to ask this lot a few questions for me, Suzie?" he asked. "You know, try to see what you can find out from the regulars who come in here?"

"Too right, I will, Inspector. What is it you want me to do?" she asked, drying her face with the back of her hand. "Just name it. I may be a glammed-up good time girl but believe me, there's a brain behind this bouffant."

Daniel smiled, warming to her in spite of her zealous greeting a few minutes earlier. "I want you to try to find out if any of Derek's friends knew who he was borrowing money from. If you manage to get a name, fantastic, but any possibilities at all would be more than I have right now."

Suzie peered through the glass at the brood of ten or fifteen men sitting along the line of TV screens. She winked at Daniel. "Leave it to me."

Daniel passed her his card. "I'm available twenty-four hours so ring me whenever you need to, OK?"

"I will. Thanks."

He nodded before gently taking Julia's elbow and leading her away from the counter. She waved a hand to Suzie to say goodbye as he ushered her back through the grimy curtain.

"What's the rush?" Julia asked. "You didn't even give me chance to say goodbye."

He turned Julia to face him. "Thanks a lot," he hissed through clenched teeth.

"What did I do?"

"It's what you didn't do," he said, nodding toward the betting shop, struggling hard to keep his grin under control.

"Oooh." She smiled, her emerald eyes glinting mischievously. "I see."

"Why didn't you warn me about her?"

She laughed. "You're acting as though she pinned you against the wall or something."

Daniel fisted his hands on his hips. "If I wasn't here investigating Derek's murder and there hadn't been a glass partition between us, she would have."

He watched her consider this for a moment before she lifted her shoulders. "You're probably right. It takes a certain kind of man to handle Suzie," she said, matter of factly. "It's not my problem if a tall, strapping detective is scared of a tiny five foot one inch woman, is it?"

"Very funny."

They stood grinning at each other, and Daniel thought she looked so happy in that moment that he would have given anything not to break it. But then she turned away and lifted a hand to her brow, shielding her eyes from the sun.

"I'd better go," she said.

He followed her gaze. "Me, too. I haven't heard anything from the team all afternoon."

Turning back to him, she smiled gently. "OK, then. I'll see you."

She pulled her car keys from her bag and stopped. "Maybe I should give you my cell phone number."

"Good idea."

She found a piece of paper in her bag and wrote it down.

Daniel resisted the urge to snatch the scrap of paper when she offered it to him, and did his best to casually stuff it in his pocket. "I'll...um...keep you updated."

"Great." Her eyes held his for a moment longer before she turned and slid into the driver's seat of her car.

****

By the time Julia arrived home the sun was beginning to set, bathing the front of her house in a warm orange glow. She walked up the garden path, pausing to pick up some fallen petals and straighten the wonky gnome. Despite the horror of the last two days, she felt strangely happy. And guilty. She knew the reason behind her sudden excitement and it meant disaster with a capital D.

Daniel, Daniel, Daniel.

A smile bubbled up inside her. He was tall and dark, kind and funny. In fact he ticked all the right boxes. She sighed. Daniel was fast becoming a third reason to climb aboard the Princess II as quickly as her size nine shoes could carry her.

Julia opened her locked front door and stepped inside. She casually threw the keys into the ceramic dish sitting on the radiator cover—and froze. Lifting her nose, she sniffed the air. Marcus. The spicy scent of expensive aftershave hung in the air like a menacing overture.

She swallowed. "Marcus?"

Nothing.

Step by careful step, she made her way along the hallway.

"Marcus? Are you in here?"

Nothing.

She glanced into the living room, the kitchen, until she finally entered the den at the back of the house.

The hairs on the back of her neck stood erect and her heart pulsed thickly in her chest. He was here, she was sure of it.

Then she saw the curtain billowing and falling on the wind from the open window and let out a frightened laugh. The scent she had smelt was stronger in here and she saw why. The bowl of pot-pours she kept on the windowsill was blown all over the room like scattered confetti.

She closed the window and knelt to sweep the mess into her hands and back into the bowl. Frowning, she tried to recall opening the window earlier that morning but couldn't. She put the bowl back on the window sill and looked around. Everything was as it should be, but still something wasn't quite right. Feeling foolish, Julia picked up the heavy paperweight on her bureau and checked behind the door and the curtains. Nothing. She released her held breath and put the paperweight back. The sooner she left town, the better.

Either that, or she'd end up in an institution.

She made her way upstairs, took off her dress and tossed it into the wash basket. Dressed in her bra and knickers, she walked into the bedroom feeling exhausted. She glanced at her watch. Having slept badly the night before, she decided to catch a couple of hours sleep before she went into work.

She lay down on the bed and closed her eyes.

"Hello, Julia."

She scrambled upright, grappling for the comforter to cover her semi-nakedness "Marcus! What do you think you're doing? How did you get in here?"

His grin dissolved. "Hey, I'm sorry, baby. I didn't mean to scare you," he said, coming closer and closer until he sat beside her on the bed.

Julia swallowed the bile in her throat. "I asked you a question, Marcus. How did you get in here?"

"You left the den window open, silly. You should be more careful. What if someone other than me got in?"

"I was just in the den and you weren't in there. Where were you?"

"I was in the downstairs bathroom. Are you all right?"

"I called out to you, Marcus. Twice."

He lifted his shoulders. "I didn't hear you. What's wrong?"

Julia stared at him, her heart racing. She had not left that window open, she was sure of it. Marcus' eyes never left hers and she had already noted the tension in his jaw. The safest thing she could do was placate him and get him out of her house as soon as possible. She forced a smile.

"Nothing's wrong. Maybe you're right. Anyway, it's shut now."

"Good, good."

"Marcus, I'm not dressed..."

He grinned wolfishly, leaning toward her, his eyes on her mouth. "I know, and you look lovely."

She curled her hands into fists around the comforter. "Would you mind going downstairs while I get dressed? Why don't you wait in the kitchen?"

Irritation quickly replaced his adoration. "I'm not going to jump on you, Julia. Why do you insist on this coy act all the time? You and I both know you act as wantonly as a cheap whore when you're at the club."

"Marcus—"

"I would have seen past girlfriends naked twenty times over in the time you've teased and tormented me these last few weeks."

"I do not tease, Marcus."

He laughed. "What do you call it, Julia? Foreplay?"

She swallowed, repulsion heating her cheeks. "I want to get dressed, Marcus. Please, will you go downstairs?"

He ignored her. "You really shouldn't have called me at the bank, Julia."

The change in subject confused her. "What?"

"It will not do for my staff to see me accepting personal phone calls."

"I didn't want to ring you, Marcus, but I had twelve missed calls from you on my cell," she said, trying to keep the tension from her voice. "It's got to stop and I could see no way of making you understand that other than calling you."

"Yes, my secretary said your tone was quite insistent. Would you convey that insistence as the behavior of someone who has lost interest in having a relationship? Or, what is it you said to me last night? Oh, yes, someone who has never had any interest in me at all?"

She sighed. The man was impossible. "Marcus, I—"

"Don't roll your eyes that way, Julia. It makes me think my being here bothers you. Like I'm a bug that needs squashing."

The tension in the air shot up a notch. Julia knew a potential explosion was brewing. She could feel it crackle in the air around her. She swallowed.

"You're right, I'm sorry. Look, why don't you wait for me in the kitchen? I'll be right down," she said.

"So now you want me to stay? You don't know how you feel about me, do you?" He smiled. "I'll tell you what, you get dressed and we'll go out somewhere."

Her stomach rolled uncomfortably. "Out?"

"We'll grab a bite to eat. How would that be?"

"I'm not hungry."

"Sure you are. You have to eat, Julia."

"I'm fine. Really."

He waved a dismissive hand in the air. "I won't hear another word. I insist. Now I'll go downstairs and leave you to get dressed."

But his facetious attitude caused her anger to claw to the surface. "Have you forgotten the note you left stuck to my window this morning?" Julia demanded. "Surely you don't expect me to have dinner with you after that?"

He slowly got to his feet. "What about it?"

"You don't think there was anything for me to get upset about?"

He shrugged. "It was just a friendly warning, that's all. I care about you."

"A warning? It was a threat."

"Julia, Julia...I think you and I need a serious talk. I'll see you in a minute."

He left the room. The lingering look he had given her before he left had made her skin icy to the touch. She would never get through to him. She had to get him out of her house. She scrambled from the bed, pulled on some clothes and brushed a hand over her hair before heading downstairs.

He sat at the small kitchen table, absently leafing through the morning's paper.

She cleared her throat. "Marcus?"

He lifted his head. "Yes?"

"Look, I agree we need to talk, but not now, OK? It's getting late. I'm tired. I want to catch a couple of hours sleep before I go into work."

The seconds ticked by like hours. He said nothing as he watched her, his gaze cold and unyielding, his lips pressed together so they showed white. Perspiration broke out on her palms but somehow she found the fortitude to keep her eyes level with his.

And then he smiled. "One cup of coffee and I'm out of here."

"But..."

"One cup, Julia."

She lingered awhile longer before she turned and flicked on the kettle with trembling hands. Julia knew from experience how close he was to losing his temper. She was not the type of girl to run from trouble, but she also had a strong sense of self-preservation. Taking on Marcus single-handedly would not be brave, but stupid.

She opened the refrigerator door. "Do you want milk or cream in your coffee?" she asked from behind the open door. There was no answer. "Marcus?"

He was right behind her, his breath hot against her exposed nape. She gripped the milk carton tighter in her hand as she slowly straightened to find his six foot frame looming over her like a dangerous phantom.

Fear beat a steady pulse at the base of her throat. "What are you doing?" she asked, forcing a laugh. "You scared the hell out of me."

"Did I, Julia? Did I really?"

She suddenly felt incredibly hot despite the cold air coming from the open refrigerator door. "Please, Marcus. You have to stop this. It's madness," she said, quietly.

"I only want to talk to you, Julia. It's not a lot to

Reluctant Witness

ask, is it?" She flinched as he took a piece of her hair and curling it around his finger. "I was hoping you were going to tell me all about the new Detective Inspector?"

She swallowed. "Inspector Conway?"

"You've been spending a good amount of time with him." He inhaled a shaky breath. "Which makes no sense to me after what happened to Phil."

She closed the refrigerator door. "Don't do this now, Marcus."

"Do what? Remind you how a cop gunned down your brother in cold blood. Mistakenly thinking him an armed robber?"

"Marcus, please—"

He dropped her hair, grasped her shoulders and spun her around. "No, Julia, no! The whole town watched your poor mother's heart be broken, saw your own hatred for the boys in blue. Now you're stepping out with one as though you're a couple?"

"I am not *stepping out* with him. I am—"

"You're what? Come on, let me hear it. What are you doing with him then?"

His face was white with anger. His face was so close to hers she could smell the scent of a cigarette on his breath. Her stomach rolled. "Look, if we're going to talk, can't we at least sit down?"

His gaze bored into hers before he took a few steps back, allowing her just enough space to squeeze past him. "Fine. We'll sit down."

She walked to the counter and filled two mugs with coffee, her hands trembling. She had to get Marcus away from the subject of Daniel. Or he would know. He'd know that she was attracted to Daniel even though it was the very last thing she wanted to be. Her mother had always said she wore her heart on her sleeve and Marcus had a way of making her slip up, say things she didn't want to say.

67

Exhaling a long, slow breath, Julia picked up the mugs and carried them to the table. Marcus took the seat opposite her.

"Well? What's his name?"

"Who?"

His grey eyes turned cold. "Don't, Julia. Don't play dumb. You and I both know you're an intelligent girl. What's the handsome detective's name?"

Surely Marcus already knew. Someone at the bank was bound to have mentioned him. Daniel probably had an account, there. Marcus was simply testing her. "Why are we talking about him? I'm more concerned with the note you left stuck to my kitchen window this morning."

"I'll ask you again. What's his name?"

Even though she risked infuriating him even more, Julia ignored his question and took a sip of coffee to ease the dryness in her throat. "You were threatening me, Marcus."

He tipped his head back, closed his eyes. "Don't be ridiculous."

"Then what did you mean by telling me not to do anything stupid?"

"Julia."

The tone of his voice and the chill in his eyes told her if she pushed him much further, there was every chance he would lose it altogether. Feeling sick, she said, "Daniel. Daniel Conway."

"Are you fucking him?"

The question was direct, unexpected and made her blood surge in her veins. "Don't be absurd. I met him for the first time yesterday. How could I possibly be sleeping with him? Didn't you just say how coy I am?"

He smiled. "I said, *act*. You *act* coy. There's a huge difference."

Her face grew hot. *You cheeky son of a bitch.*

"Whatever you meant, I am not sleeping with him. This jealousy has to stop."

He tipped his head back. "Oh, I'm not jealous, Julia." He sighed wearily. "Just concerned he has unwelcome designs on you. I've seen the way he looks at you. I dropped by the club last night. The man was literally undressing you with his eyes."

The thought that Daniel had been looking at her that way sent a fleeting sweep of female satisfaction through her but she kept her face impassive. "You have nothing to worry about on that score. Inspector Conway gave me a lift to the club because I'd left my car at the station yesterday."

His demeanor shifted and the anger dissipated. "You left your car at the station? Did something happen to you yesterday?" he asked urgently.

Again, Julia felt he was testing her somehow. Still, his seemingly genuine concern was unsettling. Manic almost—as though he were a modern day Jekyll and Hyde.

"I'm fine"

"You can't be if you had to go to the police. What happened to you?" he insisted.

"It wasn't me. It was somebody else."

"Who?" He reached for her hand on the table but she slowly slid it into her lap. His jaw tightened for a second before relaxing. "Tell me."

"It was Derek Palmer. He was killed yesterday. Murdered."

For a long moment, he said nothing and then he let out a derisive laugh. "Oh, for goodness sake!" He leaned back in his chair, laced his hands behind his head. "I was really worried someone had hurt you. Why would the fact that some doddery old man is dead be of any concern to you *or* me?"

Anger boiled over inside of her to hear him dismiss Derek's life which such nonchalance. "He was an important part of this community, Marcus!

69

He had a wife, a family. How can you be so cold?"

He smiled. "My only worry is you, my love. No one else."

She leapt to her feet. "Well, there's no need to waste any more time worrying about me. I'm not your concern and never will be."

"Sit down, Julia."

"I want you to leave. Right now."

"I said sit down."

"Your behavior towards me makes no sense. We barely know each other."

"I like you, Julia. I like you a lot, but you, on the other hand, have been determined to fight our relationship from the start."

"We went on a few dates," she cried. "It didn't work out. Most people accept that and move on."

"As will I. Once I feel you have given us the best possible chance to work."

She bit down on her bottom lip. There was no reasoning with him, none at all. She decided to try a different tactic. "I understand what you're saying, Marcus, but I will be spending a lot more time with Inspector Conway—"

"I don't think you will."

"I was the sole witness to Derek's killing. The police need my help."

He stared at her a while, and Julia's heart beat a steady rhythm against her rib cage. The tension in the room was thick enough to choke her. When he leapt from his seat, she started to scream but the sound was strangled when his hands locked around her throat. She squeezed her eyes shut. Clawed at his fingers. His putrid breath was hot against her eyelids when he spoke.

"You will *not* be spending any more time with Conway, do you understand me?" he asked, though clenched teeth. "You will stay the hell away from him."

A kaleidoscope of colors burst behind her eyelids. She tried to nod her agreement but couldn't move. This was it. This was how she was going to die. Just as the blood began to thunder in her ears, the sound of smashing glass and splintering wood pierced her fading consciousness.

Marcus released her and she sank to her knees, coughing and spluttering. She opened her eyes to see Daniel charging through her smashed back door. Marcus started to turn, but Daniel was far too quick. Before Marcus could move, Daniel had wrapped one arm around his neck in a vice-like grip while with the other he twisted Marcus' arm high up his back. Rage swirled in Marcus' eyes as Daniel wrestled him to the floor.

Julia watched in horror as Daniel deftly mashed Marcus' face against the cold tile floor and snapped on handcuffs.

"You stay right there and cool off, asshole," he said, giving him a shove. "I'm going to make sure the lady I caught you pushing around is OK, otherwise this arrest is going to get a whole lot worse."

"I was not pushing her around!"

Daniel scowled. "What would you call grabbing her by the neck?"

"Fuck you!"

"That's what I thought. You can just shut your mouth until I'm done speaking to Miss Kershaw."

"I'm not one of your average bums, Inspector. I'm a bank manager," ranted Marcus. "You'll pay for treating me like this."

"From where I'm standing, the average bum is *exactly* what you look like." Giving Marcus a final shove, Daniel stepped over him toward Julia. Her heart raced as he sank to his haunches in front of her and ran one solitary finger down her face and across her lips. "Are you all right?" His voice was gentle, his breath coming in soft pants as his

71

adrenaline slowed.

She nodded, knowing the way he was looking at her was way more personal than the usual cop/civilian consideration but not wanting him to stop. "I'm OK. Thank you," she said.

His jaw clenched as he watched her. His cocoa eyes turned to melted chocolate as they darkened. "Are you going to tell me what this was all about before I lock this moron up?"

Marcus cursed expletives behind Daniel's back as he struggled to free his hands. She looked over Daniel's shoulder and faced her demon. "This has got to stop, Marcus," she said, rubbing a hand over her raw throat. "Look what you've done. You'll be taken to the police station now. Is that what you wanted?"

He glowered at her. "This isn't my fault, you bitch!"

Daniel was on his feet in a flash. He grabbed a handful of Marcus' hair in his fist and put his face inches away from his. "Listen to me, you jerk. You're going to spend the night at the station so we can both calm our tempers. But in the morning? I'm going to make sure you pay for what you did here tonight. Do you hear me?"

"In the morning the first thing I'll do is file a charge of assault. Take your God damn hands off of me!"

"With pleasure."

Daniel opened his hand and the side of Marcus' face dropped to the floor with a thud. Julia winced and wondered how he would explain the marks on his face to the customers at the bank. She turned back to Daniel but couldn't gather the courage to tell him she wouldn't be pressing charges against Marcus. She was leaving town and she didn't need a court case, on top of everything else.

Daniel held out his hand to her. He clasped her fingers in his and pulled her to her feet. They stood facing each other in the shadowed kitchen. She resisted the urge to turn her cheek into his hand when he touched a hand there.

"I'm going to take him down to the station," he said, quietly. "But then I'll be back."

"Daniel, I've got to work tonight."

"Ring Jacob and tell him you're sick."

"I can't, he'll..."

"I mean it, Julia. Either you call him or I'll ring myself and tell him what happened here."

Julia met his gaze and blew out a breath. Her nerves were shot and her throat was sore. It would hardly be her finest hour on stage if she did arrive for work. "Fine. I'll ring him."

"Good. I'll be back in half an hour, tops."

She nodded and watched him roughly help Marcus to his feet before dragging him kicking and screaming through the house. When the front door banged shut behind them, Julia finally let the tears stinging her eyes wet her cheeks.

Chapter Five

Daniel locked the cell door behind Marcus Lowell and turned to grip the bars. Not only had Lowell dared to put his hands around the neck of his sole witness—he'd hurt the woman who, over the last forty-eight hours, had filled so much of his mind there had been little space for anything else. And now the piece of shit sat on the solitary bed, meeting Daniel's glare with cold grey eyes like he'd done nothing wrong.

"Listen to me very carefully, Lowell," Daniel said, quietly. "If I have my way, Julia Kershaw will accuse you of attempted murder when I go back to see her. If she doesn't, I'll want to know why and if I don't like what I hear, you'd better be prepared to answer a few questions."

Marcus smiled. "You're living in cloud cuckoo land if you think Julia will ever press charges against me, Inspector. We love each other."

"Don't talk such crap, you moron."

"Why don't you go ask her?"

Daniel swallowed. "I don't think grabbing a woman by the throat is demonstrating love, do you?" he sneered. "There's no way in hell Julia has feelings for you."

"Like I said, go ask her," Lowell smirked, relaxing back on his elbows. "I'll just wait right here until my brief arrives."

Daniel smiled. "Your brief? Why do you need a brief if you haven't done anything wrong?"

"I'm going to need someone to stand on the steps outside this flea-ridden pit tomorrow and explain the

74

huge police cock-up of arresting the town's most respected bank manager, that's why."

Daniel pushed himself away from the bars. "You're not the town's most respect bank manager. You're the town's *only* bank manager. There's a difference."

"Tut-tut, Inspector. Looks to me like that vein in your neck is going to pop right out if you carry on getting yourself worked up like this."

Daniel looked at the vermin in front of him. He'd wasted enough time standing here talking to Lowell. He needed to be with Julia right now.

"I'll see you in the morning. My sergeant will keep an eye on you until then. He'll contact your brief for you, too. Have a nice night."

It was nearing ten-thirty by the time he arrived back at Julia's to find the house in darkness. He slammed the car door. If she had gone to The Ship's Mate, he had every intention of going over there and bringing her home. The woman thought she was invincible, he was sure of it. He rang the bell. Once, twice, three times. Nothing.

"Damn it."

Daniel took a calming breath, then marched around to the back of the house, his arms swinging at his sides. Just as his adrenaline was about to go into overdrive, he saw her. She sat on a swing seat, plump black and white cushions pushed up all around her as she looked out toward the V of ocean he could just glimpse from her garden. He noted the furrowing at her forehead and the way she tightly clasped the steaming mug she held in her hands. He didn't want to contemplate the strong but unexpected kick in his gut as he watched her.

Almost as though she sensed him there, she slowly turned to look at him.

"You finally figured out to come round the back, then?" She smiled. "I thought Thelma had already told you I don't bother with the front door."

She was amazing. He could tell she was still shaken from Marcus' assault by the tension in her raised shoulders and the quiet sadness of her gaze, but still she smiled.

He smiled back. "Do you mind if I jump on?" he asked, nodding toward the swing seat.

She raised an eyebrow. "You certainly know how to court a girl, don't you, Inspector?"

Heat seared his face. "No, I meant..."

She tipped her head back as she laughed and when he saw the bruises Marcus had left on her throat, it took all his strength not to bolt back to the station and beat Lowell to a pulp. He swallowed his anger like a very large and bad-tasting pill.

"That's not even the slightest bit funny," he said, clearing his throat and carefully sitting down next to her.

Together, they swung for a few seconds in silence. Eventually, she spoke. Her voice soft.

"Is Marcus at the police station?"

"Yep, and that's just where he's going to stay," Daniel said. "You'll have to come down there first thing in the morning to make a statement. These things need to be dealt with immediately for the best chance of prosecution."

She put her feet to the floor and the seat abruptly halted. "Prosecution?" She paused. "Look, you may as well know I won't be any pressing charges."

"What?" He snapped his head round to look at her. "You're kidding."

Her eyes darkened. "Don't raise your voice at me. I know what I'm doing."

"He'll come after you again, Julia. Surely you know that?"

She didn't answer him and Daniel shook his head in disbelief. "The moron thinks you love him, for crying out loud."

Her eyes grew wide with what Daniel could only describe as fear. "What? He told you that?"

"Yes. And I'm guessing from your reaction, it's not true. So why wouldn't you want him standing in court for what he did to you?"

She sighed. "I've already told you, I'm leaving town soon. I don't want to have to wade through weeks of legal procedures just because he grabbed my throat. It's not worth it."

"And if he does it to someone else?"

She locked eyes with him. "That's not fair and you know it."

He lifted his shoulders. "It's still something you have to think about. The law is about people, Julia, not one person."

She squeezed her eyes shut. "I know that."

"Then why are you letting him get away with this?"

"Daniel—"

"What, Julia? What do you want me to say?"

Her eyes slowly opened. "God, what a mess." She sighed. "How did all of this happen? Last week I was relieved to have found such a great new job and the chance to get away for awhile. Now I'm caught up in a murder investigation, as well as dealing with Marcus turning into a raving lunatic."

Daniel resisted the urge to take her hand in his and instead blew out a breath. "I hate to say this, but if you know that about him, you have to press charges."

Her gaze shifted, became harder, more determined. "I don't *have* to do anything I don't want to. Marcus is upset that I don't want a relationship with him, that's all. As soon as I'm gone, he'll forget about me."

Daniel turned away from her to hide his rising frustration. "Believe what you want. It's obvious he understands you better than I do. He laughed in my face when I told him you'd press charges."

"Don't judge me. You don't have a clue what's going on with me right now."

"Then tell me. Or maybe he's right about you loving him, after all," Daniel said, sounding petty even to his own ears.

She laughed. "Don't be ridiculous. Of course I don't love him. I've told you it was me who called the dating off, let alone anything else."

He still couldn't look at her. Still couldn't stop asking her questions. "Why? What was it that made you call it off?"

"Isn't it obvious? He isn't the same person he wants the rest of Corkley Park to believe he is. Even before what happened today, I just sensed something cold in him. It was unnerving how he could turn on the charm one minute and be quiet and brooding the next."

"He hasn't been violent toward you before today?"

"No, he hasn't," she said. "I wouldn't put up with that from any man. Ever."

"And the mark on your wrist?"

She wouldn't turn her head. "That was the first time, but it was already finished between us when he did that."

"Julia, come on."

Finally, she met his gaze. "What? You think I'm lying? That he beat me?"

"No, but I want you to press charges. Get him locked up."

"No."

"Do you really think he's going to stop? I'll have no choice but to let him go in the morning and he's just going to love coming back after you and rubbing my face in it."

"Ah, so this is about you?"

He pulled back his shoulders. "Of course not, it's about you. You and the fact that I am paid to protect the innocent from being hurt by people like Lowell."

"I won't be here much longer. He can hardly get to me in the middle of the ocean, can he? As long as he doesn't find out I'm leaving, he won't know where I am."

Daniel shook his head, not wanting to be reminded of her leaving any more. "What about other women, Julia? You don't strike me as someone who doesn't care. I've seen the way people look at you around here. People do not love someone as much as they do you without good reason."

"Daniel, please. Just respect my decision."

"You're seriously not going to pursue this? You're going to let him get away with it?"

"I can't."

That word again. He'd heard her say 'can't' countless times since meeting her. This determination to escape, to deal with Derek's murder with absolute resolve instead of leaving things to the police—-the fact that she wouldn't press charges against a waste of space like Lowell. It all spoke volumes to Daniel. This had nothing to do with what was going on right now, and everything to do with her brother's death. He was sure of it.

He should know, he'd done the exact same thing for the ten years following his own father's death.

"You do understand domestic violence is an *epidemic*, a preventable disease that's taking over the country?" Daniel asked quietly. "If a guy can grab a woman by the throat, he will be capable of much more in the not so distant future."

"You're doing it again. I know this, but I will not change my mind. I can't and won't be pressing charges."

Daniel knew he should be able to control his frustration but with Lowell about to get away with grabbing her, it was impossible. "This is crazy."

"Daniel—"

"Look, you don't have to explain yourself to me. I know how these things work. He beats you, I haul his ass his jail, he gets released and then you let him back into your life. The cycle goes on because you're going to let him beat every ounce of self-confidence out of you and by the time you need me, I'll be too late to save you."

"That's not true."

"Isn't it? Do you know how hard it is for guys," he stopped, shook his head. "Sorry, cops like me to swallow the fact that sometimes we're too late?"

"Are you still talking about Marcus' attack on me today? Because if you are, you weren't too late. From my point of view your timing was spot-on."

"He still hurt you. You still have his finger marks on your neck, for God's sake. Who says next time he won't kill you? What if I'm too late then?"

He was trembling. Daniel got up from the seat before she noticed. Taking a few steps away from her, he slowly counted to ten before he heard the clink of china on stone as she placed her mug on the floor. He held himself tense, praying she didn't approach him. But God wasn't listening. She gently touched a hand to his elbow.

"Were you too late for someone else?" she asked. "Is that what this is about?"

He turned to face her, placing his hands on her upper arms. "Julia, listen to me. You're beautiful, funny, talented. Don't waste your time on a guy like that."

"I've already told you, it was over before it began. I've got this whole thing under control. I know what I'm doing. What did you mean about being too late?"

He ignored her question. "There are no guarantees in this world. Don't you get that?"

She flinched as though he'd struck her, shook off his hands. "I'm the last person on earth you need to tell about guarantees. Believe me."

Their eyes locked and Daniel's chest burned. He looked from her hair, to her eyes, to her chin and finally to her lips.

He blew out a breath. "I'd better go. I just wanted to make sure you were all right." He turned to go and then stopped, his back to her. "You're different, Julia," he muttered. "You're special. Don't ever forget that."

"I can't hear you. You'll have to turn around."

He turned and she took a step closer. Daniel's heart rate increased as he registered the way her gaze locked onto his mouth.

"I said..." he began, but the words stuck.

Did she feel it too? Did she feel this 'thing' between them? He cleared his throat. They stood just inches apart. The moon illuminated the space between them, basking her face in the soft light. Daniel could hear his own pulse beating loud in his ears. He wanted nothing more than to reach forward and pull her to him. Nothing more than to kiss those soft, inviting lips and hold her safe in his arms. How could he feel that way after only knowing her for two days? He blinked.

"I'll be in touch."

He turned and power-walked back around to the front of the house. Once he had slid into the front seat of his car, he dropped his head to the steering wheel. He hadn't been serving in Corkley Park for a month yet and now he was heading up a murder investigation and embroiled in the domestic life of the key witness.

Not only that, Julia Kershaw was doing things to his insides that no one had ever done before. Oh, he recognized the stirring further down his anatomy but the pain in his chest? That was bad. He didn't like that one little bit.

****

Four days had passed since Derek had been killed. Julia wandered down the high street with a shopping basket over her arm, feeling as helpless as she had the day Phil had been shot. She hadn't heard anything from Daniel, or any of the police, in two days, and it was driving her mad. She'd decided to drop in on Thelma, hoping she could at least provide some comfort to the elderly widow, if nothing else. The smell of the freshly baked scones drifted from inside the basket. She had also picked up some strawberry jelly and clotted cream. She'd get some flowers and spend her Sunday afternoon keeping Thelma company.

"Going for a spot of lunch somewhere, Julia?"

She jumped at the sound of Marcus' voice so close to her ear and looked left and right for the protection of other people. No matter how many times she'd told Daniel she had the situation under control, Marcus' assault had frightened her more than she'd ever admit.

People were around, but oblivious to her upset, and she seriously worried if her decision not to press charges was the right one. Not only was Marcus the town's bank manager, he was a very handsome man. It didn't matter that the devil could take any form, there was a real possibility that other women would fall for his charm and end up in the same situation.

"What do you want, Marcus?"

"You weren't there to greet me at the station doors when poor Detective Inspector Conway had to release me. I was sorely disappointed."

"I had more important things to do."

"More important than to witness my liberty and your lover's failure?"

"Daniel is not my lover and he didn't fail," Julia said through clenched teeth. "He wanted me to press charges and you and I both know you would not be standing here talking to me now if I had decided to do so."

His eyes flashed with anger. "Daniel, now, is it? Are you positive the handsome detective hasn't been inside your panties?"

Her stomach recoiled. "Don't be disgusting, Marcus."

He took a step closer. "Why didn't you press charges against me, Julia? That's the real question."

She shifted the basket and folded her arms across her chest. "Because I don't think you'll be dumb enough to try anything like that again."

"Really?"

"Really. Not with me...or anyone else."

His grin turned wolverine. "You know, you're right. I don't know what came over me, grabbing you like that. I've never touched any one in such a primitive fashion before. That's why I've come to a decision."

She narrowed her eyes. "Which is?"

"I am ridding you from my mind, Julia," he said, throwing his hands melodramatically into the air. "We obviously have an extremely detrimental effect on each other. I think it best we go our separate ways."

"I'm glad we finally agree on something," she said, then started to turn away. "Have a nice life."

His arm shot out and he gripped her hard at the elbow, his fingers pinching the flesh. "There's no need to be so final about it, darling. I'm sure we'll still see quite a bit of each other." He paused. "In fact, I'm positive we will."

"Take your hand off me right now, Marcus. You don't frighten me."

He dropped her arm. "We'll see about that. Bye, bye, then. I'll be seeing you."

Julia cursed the shaking in her hands at the

sickening realization that Marcus might just play her like a puppet until the Princess II sailed. She watched his retreating back. But what could she to do but keep dancing to each pull of his string until she left?

Her cell began to ring and she pulled it from her bag. The name on her caller ID reminded her why she had no option but to dance to Marcus' tune. Closing her eyes, she flicked open the phone.

"Hi, Mom."

"Oh, Julia. Where are you? You need to come home. I just can't cope with everything that's going on today."

Slowly Julia opened her eyes. "Why? What's wrong?"

"Your father suggested we go out for a picnic."

She said it as though he'd suggested they go skinny dipping in the ice-pools of the Artic.

Julia sighed. "What's wrong with that? That's a great idea. You could go down to the beach..."

"The beach? Oh, you're as mad as he is! I'm not ready, Julia. Why does nobody understand? No, don't answer that. I know exactly why nobody understands. It's because they haven't had their sons shot and killed."

"Dad has, Mom."

"Dad? Dad? He didn't give birth to Phil—I did!"

"That doesn't mean Phil's death meant any less to Dad. You're not being fair, Mom. We're all suffering—"

"Don't you *dare*, Julia. Don't you dare compare yours or your father's grief to mine. *Ever.*"

The line buzzed dead in Julia's ear. She closed the phone as another heavy weight dropped on top of the load already on her shoulders. Over the last six months she had watched her mother, once a strong, capable woman, slowly become a quivering, unreasonable shell of her former self. And what made Julia feel so guilty was she needed a break from it. She needed to get away before her mother's sorrow buried her, alongside her brother.

If she could just do something more to track down Derek's killer, she could leave feeling as though she'd done something to appease Thelma, if no one else. She flicked open the phone and then snapped it shut again. No, Daniel would ring her when he had any information. She had given him her number and he knew where she lived.

She would just make herself useful and try to help Thelma because God knew she was doing a lousy job of helping her mother.

A little while later, Julia sat on Thelma's sofa, watching her pour tea into bone china cups. "How are you feeling?" she asked gently.

"Oh, not too bad, dear. I've had lots of visitors. Everyone is being so kind. Your friend Suzie dropped by yesterday, and the day before. Such a big heart. Derek thought the world of her."

Julia smiled. "And she him." Her smile faded. "It was horrible telling her about his death. She knew about his debts, Thelma. Did she tell you that?"

Thelma nodded and passed Julia her cup. "She said she felt awful not telling me herself but knew it would be better coming from Derek." She drew in a breath. "This whole sad scenario is Derek's own fault, and he should've stepped up to his responsibilities and told me."

"He didn't deserve to die though, Thelma."

"No, no, of course not."

Julia watched her friend over the rim of her cup. "You look tired. Are you sleeping?"

"A little."

"Once I finish this cup of tea, I want you to try to get a couple of hours of sleep, OK? You look worn out."

"I will, dear. I will. I just wish he was still here

with me, that's all." Her voice broke.

"Oh, Thelma." Julia hastily put down her cup and pulled Thelma in close. "It's going to be OK. We'll find out who did this to Derek and when we do, they'll have us all to answer to."

An hour later, Julia closed Thelma's garden gate behind her, feeling sad and dejected. Thelma was still in an understandable state of distress and Julia knew only too well that for Thelma to have any chance of closure, she needed answers. She'd promised Thelma she would go straight to the police station and find out the current state of play.

She got into her car and started the engine. Her feelings about going to the station were mixed. On one hand she was keen to find out any new discoveries, but on the other, she was a mess of nerves at seeing Daniel again. The last time she'd seen him, standing together in her back garden, the moonlight their only witness, she'd wanted him to kiss her. To take it all away for just a few seconds.

Something had passed between them and whatever it was, it had been palpable. She'd felt as though she could've reached out and touched the connection between them like it was a durable length of twine. If she were honest, it had shocked her because she had accepted what she felt for him was nothing more than good old-fashioned lust, lust on which she had no intention of acting upon. Julia Kershaw was not, and never would be, a one-night-stand kind of girl.

She inhaled a deep breath. She'd had that little conversation with herself numerous times over the last few days. It definitely would not happen. Ever.

She pulled her car up next to Daniel's in the station parking lot and got out. Drawing herself up to her full height, Julia pushed open the door and approached the front desk. The attending sergeant met her gaze with kind, smiling eyes. She returned his smile.

"Hi, I'm Julia Kershaw. Is it possible I can speak to Detective Inspector Conway, please?"

"I'll see if he's available. Take a seat. I'll be right back."

A few minutes later, a door to her right clicked open and she turned. *Oh-My-God.* Julia clamped her lips shut to prevent her tongue from lolling out. He wore a dark, navy blue suit with a crisp white shirt left open at the collar. His jet-black hair had fallen over his brow and a five o'clock shadow faintly greyed his jaw line. His shoulders seemed to brush the wooden frame of the doorway on either side of him, making him look huge and deliciously masculine.

In short, he looked good enough to eat. In very, very small bites.

"Julia? Are you all right?"

Her heart rolled over in her chest. The deep and moving concern in his eyes made her drop her gaze to the moss-colored carpet tiles beneath her feet. Here she was, thinking what she'd like to do with some whipped cream and a very small spatula while he all he cared about was her welfare.

Shame on you, woman.

The desk sergeant silently watched them, a faint smile curling his lips. She stood and forced herself to meet Daniel's gaze. "I'm absolutely fine, Inspector," she said, aiming for breezy. "Thelma Palmer asked me to drop by to see if I could find out if you've managed to make any headway."

He stared at her for a long moment before moving closer, his manner solicitous. "There's not much I can tell you at the moment, but if you'd like to follow me back to my office..."

He left the sentence to drift off. She tilted her head, considering, then nodded and brushed past him. In his office Julia gratefully sank into the visitor's chair and crossed her legs. He walked around the desk and sat down before leaning forward on his elbows. Silently, he watched her.

Julia shifted uncomfortably under his gaze. "Why are you looking at me like that?"

"Because I haven't heard from you."

"You haven't heard from *me*? You said you'd let me know what was going on, not the other way round."

He ignored her statement. "I had to let Marcus Lowell go, Julia."

She found a spot above his head and focused on it. "I know."

"Have you seen him?"

"No," she lied.

"Are you sure?"

Her eyes shot back to his. "Yes, I'm sure. Can we stop talking about Marcus? I came here to find out information for Thelma."

"I was hoping you'd change your mind and press charges against him," he said.

"Well, you shouldn't have, because I told you I wouldn't. Can we drop this subject now. Once and for all?"

Their eyes locked and Julia found herself having to squeeze her thighs together to stop the throbbing there. He broke eye contact and lazily looked down the length of her body. Her skin burned.

"I'm here for Thelma," she said, hurriedly. "She's beside herself and from what I can tell you haven't done much to lessen her nerves."

He blinked. "I've been doing everything I can."

"And?"

He leaned back in his chair. "And that's it. I have nothing to tell you and worse, I have nothing to tell Thelma.

"But surely—"

"I am trying my best." His jaw tightened.

He looked so damn handsome all dressed up, she couldn't resist finding out why. "Your best? That must be why you're dressed up like you're going out for dinner," she said, dryly.

He slowly shook his head. "You are unbelievable."

"Thank you."

That sexy curving of his mouth appeared. "It wasn't a compliment."

"No? I'll take it as one anyway. You see, Inspector, from my experience with cops, they don't often masquerade as James Bond in the middle of a murder investigation. It smacks of bad taste."

"As much as I like the comparison to James Bond, I'm only dressed like this because I've spent the morning in court."

Heat flooded her face. "In court?"

"Yes," he said, all humor now gone. "I've been to court making sure a pedophile from the last town I was stationed at doesn't touch another child as long as he lives."

The unbearable shame started in her toes and rose higher and higher until she could feel the roots of her hair tightening. "Oh, God...I'm sorry."

He gaze was hard. "Apology accepted but please do me a favor. Stop with the assumption that the entire police force is a waste of space. We're not. Now, about Thelma..."

Julia watched from beneath her lashes as he shuffled through the files in front of him. *No, no, no—this just isn't fair. He's handsome, sexy and locking up the ultimate of the earth's scum. What next? He'll be flying all over the world, saving starving orphans? Why is it the more I learn about him, the more I want to pounce on him?*

She shook her head to clear it. "She needs to know something, Daniel. That something, anything, is being done to capture the man who killed Derek."

He wiped a hand over his eyes and blew out a tired breath. "I would love to give Thelma some good news, but the truth is I still have little to tell you. I can go over to see her later today, if you think it will help?" He put down the file in his hand and stood to take off his jacket. "I'm not avoiding her, I just don't want her to lose faith. I've told her that the next time she sees me, I'll have good news. I'm thinking maybe that was a bad idea now, but I wanted to make her understand I won't rest until Derek's killer is in custody."

He sat back down and slowly rolled back the sleeves of his shirt to reveal muscular forearms.

Julia found herself having to look away. "What about the boat? Anything on that?"

"Nope. We've checked the local marina, nothing. I've managed to get the all clear to send some officers further along the coast to check others, but that's all I can do right now. I hate to admit it, but this case could take longer than I'd originally hoped."

She snapped her head back to look at him. "How can I sail away from Corkley Parker knowing Derek's killer is still out there and I'm the only person who actually saw it happen?"

"I'll get him, Julia, it's going to take time, that's all."

"I can't stay here. I can't..." She stopped herself. *What the hell was she doing? Did she want him asking questions? Snooping into her background?*

His gaze bored into hers. "There's that word again."

She stared back at him, her lips pinched tightly together.

He leaned forward and she noticed his tone had softened when he asked, "There's more to your desperation to get out of town than Derek's murder, isn't there?"

She laughed dryly. "Isn't murder enough?"

"Please. Just tell me what it is."

"Don't, Daniel. Just leave it."

She didn't need to involve him in her problems. Whether that be Marcus or her mother. Police assistance consisted of shoot first, ask questions later. The fact that her brother's body was lying six feet under at the churchyard would always be a deep reminder of how cops worked when push came to shove.

"Look, I just wish there was more I could do to help," she said, standing. "I'll get out of your way and let Thelma know you're doing all you can."

She turned to leave but he jumped to his feet. "Wait. I was about to go to the betting shop. I haven't heard anything from Suzie. If you really want to help, why don't you come with me?"

She frowned. "You wouldn't mind me doing that?"

He lifted his shoulders. "To be honest, I'm still having trouble getting the people around here to talk to me. For some reason, I don't seem very popular and I have no idea why." He looked directly at her. "You wouldn't hazard a guess as to why that might be?"

Her stomach contracted. Did he know? How could he not? The realization left her feeling trapped—and afraid.

She hitched her bag onto her shoulder. "No idea at all, Inspector. But if I had to take a guess, I'd say it's probably due to that strange face of yours."

"What?" The furrows on his forehead deepened. "What's that supposed to mean?"

She gave a small smile, determined to mask her unease. "Oh, I didn't mean the way your nose turns the left or the fact that you have one ear slightly lower than the other," she said. "Nothing like that. I just meant people don't know you well enough yet, that's all."

He lifted a finger to his nose. "My nose doesn't turn—"

Her sudden snigger cut him off. "Come on, Daniel. Let's get out of here."

He shrugged back into his suit jacket. "You're one cruel woman, Julia Kershaw."

He came round the desk and stopped just inches away from her. Her blood immediately burned hot in her veins, heating her face and other more intimate places as she tipped her head up to look at him.

His eyes roamed languidly over her face as he said, "Even so, I'm finding it harder and harder to stay away from you."

With that, he turned on his heel and left the room.

Shock catapulted through her, leaving her glued to the spot for the next few seconds. Did he just say...? Julia closed her eyes. *This cannot be happening.*

Half an hour later Julia pulled her VW Beetle to a stop outside the betting office just as Suzie turned the sign to closed. Julia and Daniel got out of the car and approached the door.

"Suzie? Hey, Suzie!" Julia waved through the glass paneling.

Her friend looked up and Julia frowned at the nano-second of—was that panic?—that skittered through her friend's eyes before her face broke into a smile. Suzie pushed back the bolt of the door and held it open for them to enter.

"I was expecting a visit from one of you two sooner or later," she said.

Julia glanced at Daniel. Had the momentary panic in Suzie's eyes been as obvious to him as it was to her? The somber expression on his face gave no indication either way. They followed her inside and Suzie flicked a switch, flooding the room in fluorescent light.

"Suze? Is everything all right?" Julia ventured.

When Suzie turned to meet Julia's gaze, the habitual laughter now shone in her friend's eyes, although it seemed a bit strained. "Sure, honey. I'm fine. Why don't you both take a seat?" Suzie asked, hopping up onto one of the many stools that dotted the room.

Julia and Daniel sat down. Daniel pulled a notepad from his inside pocket. "No guesses as to why we're here, Suzie," he said. "Do you have anything useful for me?"

She laughed, the sound forced. "No small talk today, Inspector? Let me at least catch my breath?"

Daniel didn't laugh in return.

Suzie pointed a finger at him. "That is one serious face, Inspector. Am I in some kind of trouble now, too?

Julia touched her friend's hand. It was icy cold. "What's happened, Suze? Why are you being like this?"

Her friend pulled away. "I'm just trying to lighten him up. What's wrong with that?"

"It's wrong because you know we're here about Derek," said Julia. "Now, how about telling me what's going on? You look upset about something. What is it?"

For a long moment, Suzie said nothing, her eyes darting from Julia to Daniel and back again.

"I'm fine."

"Come on, Suzie. It's me you're talking to," insisted Julia. "What's going on?"

"It's nothing. Honestly. I'm..."

Suzie's eyes filled with tears. Julia jumped from the stool and embraced her.

"Hey, hey. Come here. Whoever or whatever has you this upset is not nothing," Julia said, holding her friend. "I can't remember the last time I saw you cry,

Suze. You're the rock of Corkley Park."

Although conscious of Daniel sitting behind them, no doubt taking in the scene and filing it for future reference, Julia didn't care one way or another. If they had to wait a little longer for Suzie's findings, so be it. Her friend's feelings were just as important right now.

Eventually, Suzie slipped from her arms. She wiped a finger under each eye, smudging glitter across her cheekbones. "It's all this business with Derek," she sniffed. "I have asked question after question to the blokes in here but every one of them says they don't know anything. I've got nowhere. I haven't found out one teeny, tiny thing to help you. I am such a big, fat, waste of space."

Julia lifted her hand to rub her shoulder. "No you are not."

"I am. Everything I do is wrong, I've got zero intelligence—"

"Suze! What's gotten into you?" cried Julia. "You're the most positive person I know. The last thing Inspector Conway wants is for you to get yourself all stressed out like this." She glanced at Daniel, but he remained tight-lipped, his notebook tapping rhythmically up and down against his knee. Glaring at him, Julia turned back to Suzie.

"Anything would have helped but if you haven't managed to uncover anything new, it's no big deal. You tried. Derek was a very private man. How were any of us to know what was really going on in his life?"

"That's just it. I did know what was going on with him and never did a thing about it," Suzie said, throwing her hands in the air. "Do you know I popped in to see Thelma the day before yesterday and the woman hasn't slept a wink in days. I can't help thinking I did that to her. What if I would have told her sooner?"

"Hey, you're going to stop this right now," said Julia, firmly. "Thelma knew what was going on. She tried to help Derek but he just got himself further and further into trouble."

"You say that, but..."

"Suzie, stop it! This isn't like you at all."

Julia snapped her head around to look at Daniel.

"It's not Suzie's fault is it, Inspector?" She raised her eyebrows meaningfully at him, but he ignored her question and continued to stare at Suzie. "Inspector?"

But Daniel kept his eyes narrowed on Suzie. "So you're telling me not one man who sits in here day after day, knew anything about Derek's situation?" he asked, quietly. "I find that pretty hard to believe, don't you?"

Julia's eyes widened. Couldn't he see the state Suzie was in? "Inspector, I really think—"

But he didn't break his stare from Suzie. "Please, Miss Kershaw, I am talking to Suzie right now."

Indignation rushed through Julia on a tidal wave. *How could he toss her aside like that? Cop or no cop, as soon as they got out of here, she'd tell him just how little she appreciated being spoken to like that.*

He slid from the stool and walked around in a circle. His eyes passed over the tobacco stained walls, the paper strewn floor and dusty TV sets. "Well? Do you believe them, Suzie? Or do you think one or two just may have a reason to lie to you?"

She nervously met Julia's eyes. "I don't- -"

He cut her off. "The one thing I've learned about addiction in my fourteen years as a police officer is that addicts seek out other addicts. It makes them feel better, it alleviates the guilt and they can feel justified in their actions. Derek was a compulsive gambler—just the same as many of the other men who come in here are. Now to my mind one of them must have said something, admitted using the same loan shark maybe, even offered to lend Derek money themselves. What do you think?"

Julia dropped her shoulders. What good would it do to be defensive? She was the one who'd been contemplating his forearms, butt and other significant parts of his anatomy, instead of questioning how Daniel Conway had managed to rise to the heady heights of Detective Inspector. Her heart beat hard in her chest.

He was the same now as when she'd be at the station looking at mug shots. She was quickly learning that his cocoa-colored eyes could be terrifying under interrogation—or as soothing as a soft caress. And the truth was as she watched him in action, Julia wasn't sure whether she felt excited or scared.

Suzie leapt to her feet. "OK, OK! Stop looking at me like that."

"Well?" Daniel leaned a little closer.

She squeezed her eyes tightly shut. "All I know is that the loan shark he was dealing with is based in Kendlewood. I haven't got a name but they're set up as a legitimate debt business." She took a few steps away from them, turned her back. "I know it's not much, but it's all I've got."

"And why would you think that information unimportant?" demanded Daniel.

"I...I..." she hung her head.

"Are you hiding something from me, Suzie?" he asked. "Because if I come to the conclusion you are, I can easily arrest you and take you down to the station for further questioning."

Snapping out of her momentary immobility, Julia jumped from the stool and rushed to her friend's side. "Suzie would never willingly hold information from the police. Tell him Suze."

But when Julia turned to her friend around, tears were sliding silently through Suzie's make-up. "All my guys are in trouble of some sort, Inspector. It makes me feel guilty that I sit in here day after day taking their money. Money they should be giving their families, not to this place."

"That's not your problem," Daniel said, matter-of-factly. "Now, look, I know you care about these men, but- -"

"Isn't it better that you now know about the loan shark?" Julia frowned at him. "I'm sorry, but it's more than you knew ten minutes ago. Can't you ease up a little?"

He turned to face her and Julia resisted the urge to take a step back.

"No, Miss Kershaw, I cannot *ease up* a little, I am investigating a murder and no one," he paused and looked directly into her eyes. "I mean, no one is going to stand in the way of my solving it."

Julia's heart picked up speed and her hands turned clammy against Suzie's shoulder. Once a cop, always a cop. She dropped her arm and pulled back her shoulders. "Fine. I'll step back and let you question your only informant how you see fit."

His eyes locked with hers. "I appreciate your understanding of the situation." He turned to Suzie. "Who told you about the loan shark?"

"What? Oh, no, don't make me tell you that," she cried, grasping his forearm. "I promised. I absolutely promised I wouldn't tell you."

"I'm sorry, but you shouldn't have done that," he said, flipping open his notepad. "I need a name."

"Inspector, please. Don't make me betray one of my boys, please."

To see Suzie this way was more than Julia could bear. She was so stressed, so unlike her usual cheerful self—it was heartbreaking to watch. Unable

97

to stop herself, Julia stepped in between them and took a deep breath. It was a sad thing to do and she was letting down the entire woman's movement but maybe, just maybe, her feminine wiles were the only weapon she had left.

She unashamedly gazed up at him through mascara-coated lashes. "Daniel, please. We have a possible lead. Do you really need to know the source in order to check it out?"

"Yes, Julia. I do." His tone was icy, but there was a new flush to his cheeks and now his jaw was clenching and unclenching. The man was faltering— well, at least Julia liked to think so.

She lifted her shoulders. "Standing here like this is wasting time. Can't we just leave for Kendlewood?"

His eyes widened. "We? Let's get one thing straight, *we* will not be going to Kendlewood, *I* will be going to Kendlewood."

Their eyes locked in battle. *Damn it. Now, I've blown my chances of a ride-along.* She threw her hands up in surrender. "Fine, but I still can't see the point in upsetting Suzie any more."

"You're unbelievable, do you know that?" he muttered.

She shrugged. "So you keep telling me. Careful Inspector, you're starting to sound like my number one fan."

Little by little, his face began to soften and Julia could have sworn she saw the corner of his mouth lift just a little. He turned back to Suzie.

"Look, you've given me a lead and for that, I'm grateful, but I still need a name."

Suzie looked from Daniel to Julia. Julia nodded encouragingly. Suzie took a long shaky breath.

"He lives on Cattlewell Avenue..."

Daniel scribbled the details into his notebook before he looked up at Suzie and smiled kindly.

"Thank-you. You did good, Suzie. You should be proud of yourself."

And with that Suzie rushed forward and pulled him into a suffocating embrace. Julia did nothing but stand to the side and hide her satisfied smile behind her hand. Suzie's massive bosom pressed up against Daniel's chest, threatening to crush his lungs.

"Oh, thank you, Inspector, thank you. I just can't cope with all this stress."

Straining to extract himself from her hysterical grip, Daniel consoled her, "It's all right. I'll tell you what, why don't you shut up shop for the night and try to get a good night's sleep?"

"Sleep? Sleep? Good God, sleep is the last thing on my mind. What I need are a couple of bottles of wine and a handsome man to share them with," said Suzie, her face serious.

Julia grinned to see at least a glimpse of the real Suzie back. "Well, there's sure to be quite a few down at the club tonight if you fancy going, Suze."

"Are you on tonight, Sweetie? 'Cause there's nothing like that smooth, velvety voice of yours to get a girl in the mood for some loving."

Julia laughed. "I'm afraid not, but Jacob's sure to have someone playing. He always does."

"It won't be the same but thanks for the tip. Let me lock up behind you guys and then I can head on home."

Chapter Six

Daniel squeezed himself into the passenger seat
of Julia's VW Beetle. Why had he agreed that she
drive? Those eyes of hers were like pools of hypnotic
liquid. One look and you were caught in her spell—
and then you lost your mind and said yes to all sorts
of stupidity. His hand sought the release under the
seat and pulled. The last person who had sat there
must have been four foot nothing.

"How you doing there?" Julia grinned.

The seat slid back and Daniel stretched out his
legs. "I'm better now."

She gunned the engine and pulled into traffic.
Daniel tapped his fingers against his knee as he
mulled over what Suzie had told him. It wasn't much
but at least he'd come away with a lead. An
unsubstantiated lead, but still a lead. His mind was
filled with the unrelenting pressure of catching
Derek Palmer's killer and figuring out what was
really going on with the woman sitting beside him.
The fact she did not want to press charges against
Marcus Lowell was a twisting knife in his gut. It had
been painful to let the son of a bitch walk out of the
station a free man.

He turned to look at her. To raise the subject
again would no doubt result in her shutters
slamming down but it was worth a try. "So what
have you got planned for your night off?" he asked,
trying to keep his tone amiable rather than
interfering. "Going anywhere nice?"

She glanced at him, her eyebrow raised. "Why
do you ask?"

He shrugged. "Just making conversation."

"Don't you want to talk about what Suzie told us back there?"

"There's not much to say for now. I'll head over to Kendlewood first thing in the morning."

"In the morning? Why not now?"

"First I want to check how many loan and debt agencies there are in Kendlewood," he said, glancing at his watch. "As it's nearing seven o'clock, I doubt there will be anyone still working at this place Suzie mentioned, anyway."

"What's your plan tomorrow? Go in and arrest whoever's in charge?"

"First I'll go down there and get a feel for the place. Check it out a little."

"Alone?"

The corners of his mouth twitched. "Yep. All alone."

"Don't you think you ought to take someone with you? You know, as back-up?"

"I'm a big boy, Julia. I'm sure I can handle this one on my own. I won't storm in there and arrest a possible suspect without any evidence of him dealing with Derek."

They pulled up at a red light and she turned to look at him. "What do you mean you have no intention of arresting him? You could be face to face with Derek's killer and you're not going to take him in?"

"I know what I'm doing. I have worked a few murder investigations in my time. Trust me, when I am positive I have found the killer, he will be arrested."

"As long as he hasn't disappeared in the time it's taken you to gather enough evidence, of course," she retorted.

His jaw tightened. "Despite your obvious lack of faith in me, I will find whoever did this. Sometimes you have to bide your time. If a suspect has no idea I'm on to him, he won't disappear, which will give me time to get sufficient evidence to ensure he's put away for the time he deserves."

"And if you're wrong?"

"I won't be."

She sniffed. "Oh, right, because cops are never wrong, are they?"

Shit. Here goes. Come on, Julia, tell me about your brother. His stomach rolled uncomfortably as he turned to look at her. "Meaning?"

"Exactly what I said. Cops are always right and if it turns out they're not, they never have to take responsibility for their actions because a judge will take their side anyway."

"You have personal experience of that happening?"

"No." Her eyes remained stubbornly on the road ahead.

"Are you sure?"

"Yes, absolutely sure."

Before he could say more, the light turned green and she pressed down on hard on the gas. They pulled away with a squeal of rubber against tarmac and Daniel decided it probably wasn't the best time to remind her of the thirty mile an hour speed limit.

"Julia?"

"Leave it, Daniel. I'm not interested."

"Fine, but let me just say this. If you're concerned about me messing up the task of finding Derek's killer, why would you let someone like Lowell just walk free?"

"Oh, my God. Are we going to go over that again?"

"Answer my question."

"That's totally different."

"I see," Daniel said, dryly. "A cold-blooded killer should be kept behind bars without question, but a guy who puts his hands around a woman's throat should be allowed to walk free, is that it?"

The temperature in the car plummeted to freezing. Her head snapped around to look at him and the glare she shot him was hot enough to heat it right back up again.

"Jerk."

"What did you call me?"

Her knuckles were white on the steering wheel as she turned back to the windscreen. "You heard me."

"Explain it to me then," he demanded, the final nuance of his patience forgotten. "Tell me why you refuse to press charges, because from where I'm sitting it makes no bloody sense."

"I don't have to explain anything to you."

"Why has he got such a hold on you?"

She let out a laugh. "You don't know me at all, do you? No one has got a hold on me, not him, not you, nobody. I know my rights. I'm under no obligation to answer your questions."

He turned to look out the window, slowly and carefully counting to ten. He seethed with anger and frustration. Part of him wanted to grab the steering wheel, turn to the side of the road and demand answers. But another, more dangerous part wanted to turn to the side of the road, take her face in his hands and kiss her long and hard.

He was mad about Lowell, but more concerned about the death of her younger brother and how her suppressed grief was going to manifest itself.

When he turned to look at her, the set of her jaw told him the best thing to do was to keep a lid on the exasperation gathering momentum inside of him. The latter half of his wishes were likely to land him into a whole load of personal and professional trouble, but the other, the answers? He considered them absolutely necessary for both her safety and sanity.

"I cannot stand by and let him hurt you again, Julia. Surely you understand that," he said, quietly.

"He won't."

"How can you be so sure? The guy's a ticking time-bomb."

"I know Marcus. He won't hurt me."

Daniel inhaled a long, slow breath. "We're not dealing with a run-of-the-mill guy here. He thinks you love him, for Christ's sake."

She indicated left and pulled into the station parking lot. "There you go, Inspector, you can get out of the car now."

He looked deep into her eyes. She was beyond angry. The gold flecks shone bright against dark emerald green. Unable to resist it, or rather her, for a moment longer, he lifted a hand to her jaw, oblivious to anyone who might see him touching a witness so intimately. She stiffened, but he didn't drop his hand.

"I won't let him hurt you, Julia. I can't." He swallowed.

Her cheeks flushed red. "He won't."

"You don't understand what I'm saying. I became a police officer for reasons you know nothing about and there is no way Marcus Lowell is going to be the man to make me break a promise I made to myself twenty-two years ago."

"Promise? What promise?"

He dropped his hand but could still feel the warmth of her skin against his palm.

"Like I said, you don't need to know."

Her eyes softened. "Daniel—"

"Tell me why you won't let me get this guy away from you."

She looked at him for a long, long time. Her teeth ground against her bottom lip as his own heart beat a steady rhythm against his chest. *Julia. Tell me. Tell me what this is all about.*

Tears shone in her eyes when she reached over and covered his hand with her own. "Marcus no longer matters. I'm leaving in six days. I know it's not necessarily the right thing to do, but I can't cope with court cases and testimony. I'm sorry. I can tell this is driving you mad, but right now I'm carrying more than I can really cope with. Please, just let me do this my way."

"I can help you. You're made of stronger stuff than you realize."

A faint smile pulled at her lips. "The human spirit can break eventually. I've seen it happen."

"To whom?"

She shook her head. "Forget it. I've already said too much. Anyway, what about you?"

"What about me?"

"What was the promise you made to yourself?"

"Oh, that. I shouldn't have said anything. Maybe you're right," he said, softly, looking out the window. "We've all got things we want to keep to ourselves."

She sighed heavily. "I may be leaving to cope with my pain, Daniel, but it seems to me you're fighting the world to deal with yours."

He turned to face her. "I am not..."

But as her gaze softened, he was tempted. Not to kiss her, but to tell her about his father's untimely death. To tell her about the violence that had occurred on the night that shaped him for the rest of his life.

But his good sense kicked in and the moment was gone. He blew out a breath. "I'd better go."

With that, he slid his hand out from beneath hers, got out of the car, slamming the door firmly behind him.

****

Julia's breath caught against the sharp stab in her chest as she watched him march through the station doors. Damn him! Damn him and this spark he'd ignited deep in her heart. A sudden wave of nausea swept through her and she quickly circled her fingers at her temples. So what if he had a secret? So what if he'd made a promise to himself that mattered enough to cause such an explosion of emotion in his eyes?

But the truth was, she wanted to go inside the station and drag him back out, demanding that he finish their conversation. She'd been foolish to let her emotions get the better of her and start ranting on about cop morality. She had a horrible, horrible feeling he already knew about Phil. The thought that he did and had failed to mention it made her feel sick—and disappointed. She wanted to believe Daniel was different than other cops, but if he knew about Phil and was withholding that information to test her...that didn't say much for his integrity.

The way he'd looked at her when he'd asked about Marcus left no doubt he was not going to let the subject drop. The same way she didn't think *she* could rest now until he shared the secret he was hiding. She slapped her hand against the steering wheel before turning the ignition. Four days she'd known him. Only four days and he was so far underneath her skin, he was making her crazy with wanting him.

She threw the car into first and headed home. She needed something chilled and alcoholic.

A couple of hours later, after a ridiculously long bubble bath that did nothing to ease the tightness in her muscles, Julia collapsed onto the sofa and aimed the remote at the TV. She flicked through the various channels. It was a toss-up between Sex and the City re-runs or a psychological thriller. She hit the off button. Being reminded of her non-existent sex life or Marcus' harassment was the last thing she needed at that moment. She rubbed a hand over her tired eyes and decided an early night would be for the best thing she could do for herself right now.

She glanced at her watch and pushed herself to her feet. Nine-thirty. Maybe she'd give her mom a quick call in the hope that she had gone for that picnic today. God willing, she had actually managed to have some semblance of a mediocre time.

"Hey, Mom. It's me."

"Hello, darling. I'm so glad you called. I'm sorry."

"For what?"

"For shouting at you earlier today. I shouldn't have done that."

Julia gave a small smile. "That's OK. It's forgotten. You sound a lot better than you did. Did you go for a picnic after all?"

"No, no we didn't, but I did sit out in the garden," her mother said. "Mind you, Lord knows what the neighbours thought because your father insisted on having the picnic on the lawn. He even opened a bottle of wine."

Julia smiled. Her dad was a man of complete and utter determination. He would get her mother through this—even if Julia couldn't. "Well, that sounds pretty romantic to me, Mom."

"Romantic? Oh, Julia." Her mother sighed. "I think I'll go to bed now."

"What's wrong? What did I say?"

"I'm trying with you, Julia. Really, I am, but sometimes I wonder if you have the slightest clue about real life. Your head is in the clouds, filled with daydreams and thoughts of being a singer."

"That's not fair, Mom, and you know it."

"Do I? At least your brother—"

Julia cut her off, tears threatening to fall. "I can't handle this any more, Mom. Ever since Phil died, you seem to blame me, direct all your anger at me. Why? What the hell did I do?"

"Don't you raise your voice at me, young lady..."

The door bell rang. "I've got to go, Mom. There's somebody at the door."

"Well, isn't that convenient."

"Mom, please, don't do this."

"Bye, bye, then. I'll see you when you can find the time to come round before you take off around the world."

The doorbell rang for a second time and Julia slowly hung up the phone. The doorbell's shrill insistence made her hackles rise. Oh, yes, she was ready for a fight. Her mother had seen to that. She took a determined step toward the door, then stopped.

Who could it be at this time of night? Marcus? Her shoulders tensed and her heart picked up speed.

"Hello?" she demanded, forcing false bravado into her voice. "Who is it?"

"Julia? It's me."

Daniel.

She looked down at her crumpled cotton pajamas. *Great. Now he wants to talk.* Cursing continually, she yanked the scrunchie from her hair and pulled the Homer Simpson slippers from her feet before throwing them behind the sofa. She touched a hand to her face, naked of make-up. *Oh, for goodness sake. Get a grip. What does he expect when he turns up unannounced?*

Lifting her chin, she walked purposefully to the door. The man was a cop, not a date. Who cared what he thought of her sleeping attire, or her house, for that matter? She threw back the bolt and opened the door.

A bag of Chinese takeaway greeted her. She couldn't fight her grin or ignore the way her heart flipped over in her chest. He peeked around the side of the bag.

"Hungry?" he asked, his boyish grin roguishly

wide.

"You'd better come in." She stepped to the side, wanting him to go first, so he didn't see her butt in her saggy pajama bottoms. "The kitchen's through there."

He brushed past her and Julia nodded appreciatively at his rock hard butt. *Oh, yes, far better to be the viewer than the viewee.* With an unconscious skip, Julia followed him into the kitchen.

"I assumed the reason for this visit would be more unwanted questions, not to ply me with Chinese food," she said.

"I hope the food is a better option." He smiled and dumped the bag on the kitchen table.

"Absolutely, you'll hear no complaints from me." Their eyes locked for a moment and Julia vowed that whatever happened in the next hour or so, she would not ask him about The Promise. No way, no how. That particular ball could remain firmly in his court. "So..." she said. "Did you manage to track down any debt agencies in Kendlewood?"

"Two. I'll run down there in the morning and check them out."

She pulled some plates from the cupboard and laid them on the table while Daniel busied himself sorting out the various boxes, chopsticks and napkins.

"I wasn't sure what you liked so I pretty much ordered everything," he said, a hint of color staining his cheeks.

Julia laughed. "I can see that. How much food did you buy? There's enough here to invite the neighbors over for something too."

He grinned. "I'm sure we'll get through it if we try hard enough."

Julia swallowed. It felt so normal to have him there, standing in her kitchen, spooning egg fried rice onto a plate already steaming with sweet and sour chicken. She discreetly drank him in. Her gaze traveled down his torso, over his ridiculously muscular thighs, right down to his sock-covered feet...

Her eyes widened. "Where are your shoes?"

"I left them on the doorstep."

"What? How did you know I'd even be in?"

He shrugged. "If you weren't, I'd have just put them back on again. No big deal."

She bit back a laugh. "Do you always do that?"

"It's the polite thing to do in other people's homes, don't you think?" he asked, sucking sauce from his finger. "Now, where are your wine glasses?"

Julia was contemplating how amazingly adorable a six-foot-two man could suddenly look in just his socks, when she caught the way he was watching her. "What?" she asked.

"You're doing that zoning out thing again." He smiled.

"Am I?" she asked, her face suddenly warm. "Do I do it often?"

"Not really," he said, taking a step toward her. "It only seems to happen every now and then when you're looking at me."

He took another step closer and Julia shot past him to the cupboard where the wineglasses were kept. She flung open the door and held the glasses aloft like trophies.

"Ta-da!" She panted. "We have glasses."

He moved to the side, that annoyingly sexy smile still on his face. She filled the glasses with the smooth, Cabernet Sauvignon he'd brought, and they carried their drinks and overflowing plates into the living room. Side by side, they sat down on the settee.

"I'm guessing you like candles?" Daniel said, glancing around the room.

Feeling more than a little self-conscious, Julia laughed. "They help me relax." She'd lit at least twenty of the damn things tonight.

"I'm all for that." He smiled at her. "Tuck in. I expect to see a completely clean plate."

"I'll try."

As soon as the first mouthful touched her tongue, Julia realized just how hungry she was. When Phil had died, she'd lost nearly thirty pounds and had looked like an extra from Michael Jackson's Thriller video. She did not want to go down that road again under the pressure of Derek's murder and Marcus' increasingly erratic behavior.

She stole a glance at Daniel as he struggled to pick up some noodles with his chopsticks and smiled. She felt safe with him sitting beside her and her appetite was back with a vengeance.

"Fancy swapping a spring roll for a prawn cracker?" she asked.

He picked up a cracker and surprised her by putting it to her lips. She let him feed her before turning back to her plate, resolutely refusing to think anything else was happening here other than two people sharing a meal. They spent the next twenty minutes exchanging odd bits of conversation, purposefully steering away from Derek's murder, Marcus, and each other.

Julia pushed her empty plate onto the coffee table and thanked God for the elasticized waistband of her pajamas. "Phew, I am stuffed!"

Daniel laughed. "You finished the plate though. My mission is complete."

"How could I not? It was fantastic."

He scraped up the last grains of rice on his own plate before leaning forward and placing it on top of hers. He reached for their glasses of wine and passed one to her.

"Here."

"Thanks." Their fingers brushed and Julia felt a bolt of electricity rush through her. The atmosphere was intimate, the mood shifting. There were so many things she wanted to know about Daniel Conway. The man, not the cop. Her mother's tear-stained face filled her mind and the guilt she felt for really beginning to like and respect this man stole grasping fingers around her heart. She took a sip of wine, and laid her head back against the sofa. She watched his profile as he looked around the room and blinked back the sudden burning behind her eyes.

She knew she was heading for trouble. Terrible, potentially explosive trouble. How could she possibly contemplate kissing a cop? Her mother's heart would never recover. She cleared her throat. Maybe she *should* ask him about the promise. Maybe it would push him far enough away that he withdrew from her completely.

She turned to look at him. "What did you mean earlier? When we were talking in the car?"

He didn't look at her. "When?"

"You know. The Promise."

He took a sip of his wine before slowly exhaling. "Oh. That."

"Yes, that. You looked so...angry...no, sad. Oh, I don't know. But it definitely wasn't anything to do with me and Marcus. It was more personal than that, wasn't it?"

His broad shoulders immediately tensed high around his neck and before she could stop herself, Julia reached out a hand and gently touched his arm. "Daniel?"

He dropped back against the settee alongside her. You're right. It was personal. No, it *is* personal."

He turned to meet her eyes and her heart kicked against her ribcage in one swift jolt to see such torment.

"What happened?" she asked, quietly.

"My father was murdered."

"Murdered?" she whispered.

"Murdered. Shot through the heart with a single bullet."

"Oh, my God. I am so sorry." She moved her hand and let it cover his, as it lay limp on his knee.

"I was nine years old. He'd pushed me inside a cupboard so the men who'd come after him wouldn't know I was there. They shot him in cold blood as I watched through a gap in the cupboard doors. If I close my eyes I can still hear the sound of the shot and the crack of wood as my father fell against the door."

Julia squeezed his hand. "Oh, God. I don't know what to say."

He tried to smile. "There's nothing you can say. That day I vowed to become a cop just like him."

"He was a cop?"

"Yep, and a bloody good one. Just maybe not good enough to prevent getting himself shot." He continued to look at her. "I was eighteen when I signed up. I worked hard, kept long hours until I was finally promoted to detective at twenty-two. Made my mother's day to see me."

"Does she live close by?"

"She goes where I go. Afraid of something happening to me, I guess. If I'm re-located, she comes too. I'd love her to meet a special someone for herself one day, shift the focus from me a little." He smiled but Julia could tell it was hard for him. "But I don't think she will, I never known her to even look at another guy my whole life."

Julia sighed. "The one thing I know for sure is you should count your blessings if true love shows up in your life once, let alone twice."

He turned her hand over and stroked his finger along the pale yellow bruising on her wrist.

"Absolutely."

She shivered involuntarily at the way his eyes lingered with hers just a little longer than necessary. She swallowed and gently pulled her hand from his grip.

"You know, my parents are still as deeply in love as the day they married. Maybe more so. My mom is having a few difficulties right now, but I know they're going to be OK. I used to watch them and wonder how love like theirs was possible, but it is. They would laugh like teenagers and pull funny faces at each other when they thought nobody was looking."

"So what happened?"

She frowned. "What do you mean?"

"You said your parents are still in love but then changed to past tense."

"Did I?"

He nodded. "You said, they *used* to laugh and joke."

Unable to look at him, she closed her eyes. "There's something you don't know about me. Something that happened to me and my family."

He shifted his weight so he directly faced her and Julia felt perspiration break out cold on the back of her neck.

"I'm listening," he said.

She squeezed her eyes closed, not quite believing she was about to tell a cop, of all people, about Phil's death. When she opened her eyes and met his gaze, that inexplicable security settled over her like a well-worn comforter.

"My brother died just over six months ago," she began. "There hasn't been a lot of laughter in my mother's house since that day. He was mistaken for a robber holding up the garage. He was shot dead...by a cop."

Her whoosh of released breath sounded loud in

the room. He took her icy cold hand in both of his. "I know, Julia."

She nodded. "I sort of guessed as much."

"I wanted to hear it from you. I'm sorry."

Julia waited for the outbreak of her stored anger, the release of indignant affront, but it didn't come. Instead she felt the tiniest lifting of weight from her soul. It was not an enormous amount, but it felt significant—as though Daniel had taken a small piece of her endless grief and put it onto his shoulders in an effort to help her.

"I understand." She smiled tentatively.

"You do?"

"Uh-huh. There's something inside me that needed to hear your promise, too."

"A secret for a secret?"

"Something like that."

His shoulders relaxed a little. "I didn't immediately link your name with your brother's, although I should have. I'm so sorry you're going through this."

"Thank you."

"So...what about you?" he asked. "How are you?"

Her heart contracted. "I'm fine."

"Julia."

"Come on, Daniel, I've told you about Phil, but I won't be talking about my own feelings any time soon, OK?"

"With me? Or with anyone?"

She swallowed. "With anyone."

He picked up his wine glass and took a gulp. "I promised myself I would never let another killer walk away like my father's did."

"Your father's killer was never found? Not even after all this time?"

"Nope, and the likelihood is he never will be. Too much time has passed. That's why time is of the essence in Derek's case."

Julia felt sick. She was the sole witness and she couldn't even describe Derek's killer to him. "I feel so useless. If only I could have made out the killer's face, or the name of the boat. Something."

"We'll find him, Julia."

"But the guy could be half way round the world by now."

"We'll find him."

His soft, velvety gaze wandered over her hair, her eyes, her lips. They glimmered with intensity and her skin hummed with the burning need to be touched. She suddenly craved the feel of his fingers edging over her body, the heat of his tongue inside her mouth.

The words were out before she could stop them. "Will you kiss me, Daniel?"

He hesitated. "Kiss you?"

She nodded.

And then he took her wineglass and put it on the coffee table with his own. Her heart beat a wild tattoo in her chest. He turned, faltered for a second, then cupped her face in his hands. Her eyes flickered closed as he leaned toward her. She felt the soft warmth of his breath and the gentle caress of his thumbs as he drew them across her closed lids.

The sofa creaked faintly under his weight as he moved closer, and Julia slowly opened her eyes. He was still watching her, his gaze slowly gliding over her face. How could one man's attention make you feel so incredibility beautiful? The corners of his mouth lifted.

"I think you're pretty wonderful, do you know that?"

She laughed quietly. "I thought you were going to kiss me, not look at me."

"I am. I will."

His lips were warm against hers. She watched his eyes drift shut and felt the soft whisper of his possession. Her own body relaxed into submission as her fingers smoothed up over the thick span of his bicep to grip his shoulder. Brazenly, she pushed her tongue into his mouth. She wanted to tease, to play, to feel his increasing arousal.

The kiss was so natural. It built slowly, the flames flickering, catching and then burning before dying back and re-igniting again. Julia clung to him, gratefully pulling his weight against her. She was aware of his huge hands spanning her waist and enjoyed the rare sensation of feeling so small.

More for the need to catch her breath, than wanting to end the kiss, she slowly pulled away. Their breathing was now a little faster than before. She opened her mouth to say something but Daniel spoke first.

"I'll more than likely get fired if anyone finds out I did that but right now I couldn't care less," he said, smiling softly in the shadow of the candlelight.

She gently laughed. "Believe me, if my mother could see us, another murder would be committed."

He brushed a stray curl from her cheek. "That protective, huh? Understandable, I suppose."

"Something like that."

Julia pursed her lips together to stop herself from saying more, and for a long moment they sat looking at each other.

"Do you want another glass of wine?" she asked, tentatively.

He blew out a breath. "No, I'd...um...better be going. Early start in the morning."

When he stood, she did too. She wanted to tell him to stay, to go upstairs with her right now and finish what they'd started, but it was impossible. He was right. He could lose his job and she would break her mother's heart. She stooped to pick up their glasses, anything to avoid looking at him.

With amazing clarity it smacked her between

the eyes, that she was teetering on the edge of a deep and endless abyss. Barely a step away from falling into it, hard and head first. She could not risk looking into his eyes, seeing he felt the same overwhelming desire.

But the fight was fruitless. She needed to see, needed to know. When she finally lifted her head, it was clear Daniel's thoughts were far from mirroring her own. He looked afraid.

"I'll call you tomorrow," he said.

"Sure." She plastered a smile on her face before walking from the room and into the hallway. The light above them was far too bright and glowed like an unwelcome spotlight.

Julia bit down on her bottom lip when he bent to put on his shoes. The thought that she might never be drawn to someone like this again suddenly frightened her more than any threat from Marcus or her mother could.

He straightened. "Thanks for a wonderful night."

"Daniel?"

"Yes?"

She hesitated. "Thanks for the food."

"You're welcome."

He stepped forward and kissed her cheek before he turned and walked out the door.

Chapter Seven

Daniel awoke to find his bedroom flooded with another morning of bright sunshine. For a few seconds he lay peacefully awake, the previous night escaping his memory. But as he stretched his arms above his head, the memory returned and crashed into him like a demolition ball.

He pulled the pillow over his face and groaned.

The groan wasn't from regret. Nor was it the sound of a man waking from a night of bad decisions and too much tequila. Daniel Conway groaned from the realization that he might have just plonked his heart down right in front of Julia Kershaw like an offering on a silver platter.

Her lips had tasted like nothing he'd ever sampled before. She was so...He grinned...so bloody sexy. Her eyes drew you in, her scent tempting and provocative, but her kiss? Jesus. He felt himself grow hard beneath the cotton sheets and grimaced. How old was he? Fourteen? God, this was bad.

She had bashed headlong into his life and now he felt as though he'd do anything to keep her there. He wanted to hear her laugh, hold her when she cried, listen as she told him about her life, in fact, learn every little thing about her. He swallowed, hard. For the first time in his life, there was a real possibility he could be falling in love.

The only snag in this happily ever after? Julia Kershaw was the key—no, the only—witness his murder investigation. It wasn't professional and God knew he had *always* been professional.

He leapt from the bed and into the bathroom. He

needed to take a freezing cold shower before he completely lost his senses.

An hour later he had checked in at the station and was on his way to Kendlewood. A bigger town than Corkley Park, people came to Kendlewood to either work, shop or do business. It did not echo with laughter, fun and the good times of its seaside neighbor. Both towns were under Daniel's jurisdiction but as far as Daniel was concerned, the sooner he got back to Corkley Park, the better.

He'd pre-planned this trip and knew exactly where the Dial-A-Debt office was situated. He pulled to a stop outside and pushed open the door. He walked into a plush, white-walled office with little decoration and even less personality. A tall, dark-haired man in his late thirties rose to his feet from behind one of the two desks.

"Richard Bainbridge, how may I help you, sir?" he asked, flashing a bright white smile and extending his hand.

Daniel barely shook his hand before pulling his ID from his inside pocket. "Good morning, I'm Detective Inspector Daniel Conway. I'm here on official police business. I'm hoping you will be able to help me."

"Well, yes, yes, of course, Inspector," Bainbridge said, smoothing back his hair with a brush of his hand. "Won't you have a seat? Tea? Coffee?"

Daniel sat and studied the man in front of him. Vain was the first word that leapt to mind. His clothes, hair and manicured hands left little doubt this guy took personal grooming very seriously. "Coffee would be great." Daniel looked around. "Does anyone else work here? It seems kind of quiet."

Bainbridge walked over to a small table holding tea and coffee making facilities. He picked up the aluminum coffee pot and filled a cup for each of them. "Um, yes, my secretary Gillian, but she's out sick today, I'm afraid. Is it her you've come to see?"

Daniel raised an eyebrow. "Why do you ask?"

He shrugged. "No reason."

"No, Gillian is not the reason I'm here," Daniel said. "I'm sure you'll be able to help me as much as your secretary could."

"Oh?" he said, passing a steaming cup to Daniel.

"I'm looking for any record you may have of a Mr. Derek Palmer. Do you recognize the name?"

"Derek Palmer?"

Daniel watched as Bainbridge looked off into the distance. When he turned back and met Daniel's eyes, his gaze was cool. Calm.

"No, no, I can't say I do. I'll check for you though. How long ago do you think he may have used our services, Inspector?"

"If you could check over the last twelve months or so." Daniel deliberately paused. "For now."

"Right. Right. Is there a number I can call you on?"

Daniel smiled and leaned further back in his seat.

"I'm quite happy to sit here and wait. If it's all right with you."

Color rose in the other man's face and Daniel smiled inwardly. *Maybe not so cool after all.*

"Of course. No problem at all, Inspector," Bainbridge said, stiffly.

He began tapping away at his computer, running his finger down the screen, getting up from his seat once or twice to check the filing cabinet. Finally after twenty minutes, he said, "Nothing, I'm afraid. There is no Derek Palmer on our records. I took the liberty of checking back two years. Nothing."

Daniel blew out a breath. "OK, could you print off a copy of all your clients over that period and let me take them with me? He may have been using an alias."

"Everything we hold on file is extremely confidential..."

Daniel sighed and drew out his cell phone. "I can obtain a warrant if needs be."

Their eyes locked for a long moment. Then Bainbridge turned back to the computer, tapped a few keys and the printer began throwing out pages. He gathered the papers and handed them to Daniel.

"You might want to try Lawson's at the other end of town," he suggested. "And the bank, of course. Money can be borrowed in any number of places in this town, Inspector."

Daniel nodded. "I appreciate that, Mr. Bainbridge. Lawson's is next on my list. Thanks for your help."

"Not at all."

Daniel nodded curtly before turning and heading out the door.

Lawson's was as much a waste of time as the bank was afterward. It appeared Suzie's informant was completely off the mark. Whomever Derek had been getting the money to gamble from, they were not located in Kendlewood, unless it was a completely independent source, or worse, an underground organization. Daniel's stomach knotted uncomfortably. He didn't even want to contemplate going down that route. His phone vibrated in his pocket.

"DI Conway."

"It's me."

He felt a grin emerge like magic. "And how are you this morning?"

"Great, how are you?"

She sounded shy, and Daniel's smile widened. "Great."

There was a pause. "I was wondering how you got on

with the debt agencies. Any luck?" Julia asked.

"Nothing, but I'm not giving up yet."

"Does that mean you have a plan B?"

"In fact, I do," he said, and wondered when his plan had somehow miraculously included her. "Coincidentally, it involves you."

"Oh? How?"

"I need your help again. Do you mind?"

"Mind? God, no, I'm desperate to help. After you...um...left last night, I was pretty sure my involvement was no longer needed."

Daniel lifted a hand to his forehead and squeezed his eyes shut. He'd left abruptly because if he'd stayed one minute longer, he would've ripped those spotted pajamas from her body and taken her right there in the hallway. The raw animal need that had pulsed through his veins like molten lava had frightened the hell out of him.

"I rushed off because I'd lost all track of time and wanted to make an early start this morning," he said, feebly. "This investigation is my priority right now."

Another long pause. "But of course it is. Mine, too. The Princess II sails in five days and the last thing I want is to leave knowing Derek's killer is still out there somewhere."

Daniel sucked in a breath against the unexpected stab in his chest. The truth of it was he was a fool for thinking about any possibility of a future with her. He might as well get used to the idea that after the end of the week, the next time he'd see Julia Kershaw she would be sitting in a witness box.

"Daniel? Are you still there?"

He forced a smile into his voice. "Still here. Listen, where can I catch up with you? We need to put this plan into action."

"I'm going to the Cove if you want to meet me

123

there. I don't want to avoid the place forever. It's been special to me for too long."

Daniel looked up at the azure blue sky. The sun burned brightly, the day heating to the predicted eighty degrees. He closed his eyes. A perfect day for joining a lover at the beach in his swimming shorts rather than on police business. *Dream on, Buddy.*

"I'll see you at lunch time and fill you in on your next assignment, OK?" he said.

"Great. I'll bring the food."

"Food?"

"Well, I thought, no, forget it," she mumbled. "Bad idea."

"What?"

"I thought we could, you know, make it a working lunch? Just a sandwich, nothing fancy."

"That sounds great."

"It does? I mean, good, that's good. OK, I'll see you at twelve-thirty, then."

She hung up and Daniel stood staring at his phone, knowing there was no turning back. He'd fallen for the last person he had any business falling for.

****

Standing in front of the mirror, Julia eyed herself critically. The black bikini felt too safe but the red too obvious. The real question was why she was trying on a bikini in the first place? She was meeting a police officer to discuss the subject of murder. With a groan of frustration, she stripped off the bikini and threw it on the bed. If she could get the fantasy of Daniel's hands on her body out of her head for one lousy second maybe she wouldn't be so intent on baring all.

She finally settled on a strappy pale pink vest top and white cotton shorts. She tied her hair back from her face with a pink bandana and slipped on white leather flip-flops. She may have looked suitably cool and casual, but her insides were alive with guilty——and fiery—excitement. They'd connected last night. She'd felt it, and was convinced he had, too.

After a night of little sleep and a whole lot of thinking, Julia had decided maybe running away wasn't the answer to her problems. Daniel Conway had become important to her. It felt sudden, inappropriate even, but who was to say he wasn't the man she was meant to be with? What if there was a real possibility he and she could have what most people never found their whole lives?

She picked up the brochure sitting on her bureau. Its glossy cover boasted the thrills and relaxation of four months aboard the Princess II. Honeymooning couples and elderly companions relaxed under a blazing hot sun. In the background, children wearing clown noses and painted faces laughed and played in the brightly decorated kids' clubs.

Just a short few days ago, Julia had thought this was the perfect escape route from both her mother and Marcus. Now the idea of leaving made her resent them both. She didn't want to leave any more——at least not yet. Not until she was certain this hunch she had about Daniel was more than good old-fashioned lust.

Should she ring and resign from her position on the ship right now? The most poignant lesson she'd learnt from her brother's and Derek's senseless death was that life was as fragile as the human heart. Julia reached for her cell and opened the front page of the cruise brochure. She was probably too late to break her contract, but it was worth a try.

Before she could dial, the phone rang. For a long moment, Julia just stared at the number on the display. She was in such a fragile, nerve-jumping place at that moment she was unsure if she could take another barrage of abuse from the person on the other end of the phone. Drawing in a breath, she pressed talk.

"Hi, Mom," she said, quietly.

"Before you say anything, I'm ringing to apologize. I shouldn't have hung up on you last night, darling."

"It's fine, Mom. Don't worry about it."

"No, no it's not. Your father made me realize while we were lying awake last night that I haven't even asked how you are feeling since witnessing poor Derek Palmer's murder. I'm so sorry, sweetheart, really I am."

"I'm fine, Mom. Honestly."

"But how can you be? To see such a thing. To be personally involved in two senseless shootings in a year. It's unheard of, Julia. Your heart must be in pieces—"

"Mom, listen to me. The police—"

"The police? Please tell me you're not putting your faith in them doing the right thing and bringing Derek's killer to justice," she said, coldly. "They're nothing but selfish, cold-hearted, evil, gun-shooting murderers, the whole lot of them."

Her voice cracked and Julia felt the heavy weight come crashing down once more on her shoulders. "Mom, this has got to stop. One minute you ring me to apologise, the next you rant and rave at me for something that is completely out of my control. I refuse to keep letting you do it, Mom. It's not fair."

"Now, you listen to me—"

"I hate upsetting you, but would you rather lie to you?"

"Of course not, and I'm not upset, Julia. I'm angry. I don't want you to ever lose sight of what the police are, that's all." She sighed. "You're a good girl. I should've guessed that they'd get to you too, eventually."

Julia squeezed her eyes shut. To hear such imbedded animosity spewing from a woman who six months ago would have stepped in as mediator between anyone involved in the smallest of disputes was so hard to listen to. She let out a long breath.

"Do you want to come out for a bite to eat with me tomorrow, Mom?" she said, pressing her fingers to her closed eyelids. "We could go—"

"Oh, I see. You want to take me out one more time."

"What do you mean, one more time?"

"Before you leave me here all alone and go off around the world. A farewell lunch, you might say."

"I'm hardly leaving you all alone. Dad will be here, Mom," Julia said, deep down knowing her father was no longer enough. None of them were. She opened her eyes. "Let him get close to you again, Mom. He loves you. Phil isn't coming back and you have to try and accept that. You'll never forget him but he wouldn't want you to be like this."

Margaret Kershaw's breath hitched. "You don't understand."

"I'm trying to. I lost a brother and it hurts so much but I know it is not the same as losing a child. I just don't know what to do to help you, Mom."

A somber silence stretched over the line. Julia felt warm tears on her cheeks as she listened to her mother's breathing hitch and release.

Finally her mother spoke. "Oh, I'm sorry, sweetheart. Really, I am. Can't you come over this afternoon? I need to see you. I can't bear being in this silent house all day, every day."

Julia pulled her hair back in a fist as Daniel's face rose into her mind's eye. "I have a meeting with Inspector Conway, Mom. I can't."

"You're meeting with the police?" Her mother's voice was dangerous low.

Rachel Brimble

Julia swallowed. "Yes. I am."

"You've lost your mind."

"I've witnessed a murder. I have to cooperate as much as I can." She paused. "I want to help them find Derek's killer. Is that so wrong?"

There was a long pause and if Julia wouldn't have heard her mother's shaky breath, she would have thought she had put the phone down.

"Mom?"

"Fine," Margaret said with a sigh. "Do what you have to. But don't you forget for a second they killed your brother, Julia. *Killed* him. My heart goes out to poor Thelma losing Derek like that but I will never, ever trust a policeman again as long as I live."

And that sealed the lid on any ideas of pursuing a relationship with Daniel. How could she even think for one second they would have any sort of future? It would be like flaunting Phil's death in front of her mother every time she set brought him to the house.

"Julia? Are you listening to me?"

"Yes, Mom. I heard every word."

"Good. Because I hate every last one of them."

Ten minutes later, Julia dropped the receiver into its cradle and collapsed back onto her bed, exhausted. Everything was closing in on her. Her mother, the murder, Marcus. The hum of sexual tension between Daniel and her was hardly enough to make her entrust her heart as well as her belief in a man who carries a gun each and every day. Heaving herself to her feet, Julia turned the cruise brochure face down and picked up her bag. The sooner she found what she could do to help with the investigation, the better. She had to leave—-her growing feelings for Daniel could no longer be a deciding factor.

The beach was packed with holiday makers. School had finished for the summer and people from all over the UK had traveled south to catch the best of the sun. Julia weaved among them as she made her way to the Cove. But when she reached the final boulder which served as the entrance, a brutal and sudden wave of nausea struck her.

The moment Derek was shot flashed clear and vivid in her mind. The memory of his limp body being tumbled overboard brought a hand to her open mouth. She gripped the boulder as the sand shifted beneath her feet. His killer was still out there, running free. Squeezing her eyes shut, Julia waited for the dizziness to pass. She could not allow the killer to take her Cove as well. Opening her eyes, she hitched her bag higher onto her shoulder, and continued to march resolutely across the sand.

She came to a quiet, secluded spot, dropped her bag and the picnic basket onto the sand. Shielding her eyes against the sun, Julia stared out toward the horizon. Death might have taken Derek, but it couldn't take away the way the sun shone upon the water or the feel of its rays upon her face. Corkley Park was her haven, the place where she had grown up and never felt afraid, but in the last six months, everything had changed.

She heard crunching sand behind her. She turned and her stomach gave a jolt. Daniel.

He raised a hand. "Hey."

"Hey."

Her heart picked up speed as he walked toward her. She swallowed and turned back to the water.

He came to a stop beside her, his bicep brushing her shoulder. "How are you doing?" he asked, quietly.

She had to tip her head back to look at him. "Fine. You?"

His eyes met hers and he smiled. "All the better for seeing you."

Heat seared her cheeks and she laughed softly.

"Corny, Inspector Conway. But still nice."

He pressed his hands to his chest. "Give a guy a break will you? It's been a long time since I did this stuff."

She arched an eyebrow. "What stuff?"

"You know."

She couldn't help teasing him, even though deep down she knew she should not be flirting with him. "You mean I'm not the first girl you've wooed this way?"

He laughed. "Wooed? When were you born? 1810?"

She punched him playfully on the arm. "Hey!"

"I'm wooing you? Who uses words like that anymore?"

"I do. OK?"

As he stared down at her, Julia could see the rise and fall of his chest, moving strangely in time with her own.

"What are you thinking?" she asked, noticing the sudden sadness that clouded his eyes.

He brushed the hair from her eyes. "That I'm a cop and I shouldn't do what I'm about to do."

His lips were warm against hers and so tentative, Julia barely dared to breathe. She was aware they were playing a dangerous game, and if Daniel was feeling half of what she was, they would both soon be left with a cold and empty void in their hearts. Daniel was tough and capable, kind and funny. He was everything she wanted and now that she'd found him, she would have to let him go...

Abruptly he pulled away from her. "Are you crying?"

She swiped the tears from her cheeks, unaware they had fallen. "Of course not."

"Julia—"

"Daniel, please. I can't talk about it."

"Can't or won't?"

She met his eyes. "You're right. We shouldn't be doing this, allowing this to happen. There's no point to it."

"No point to it? I agree we're not the best combination on paper. Cop and witness but in here..." He took her hand and pressed it to his chest. "In here, there is definitely a point to this."

"But my mother—"

"What about her? If I'm willing to face everything my governor will undoubtedly throw at me, surely you can face your mother?"

"It's not the same, Daniel. A cop killed her son. She will never, ever accept you. She told me less than an hour ago how she hates all cops. She was so sincere, it was scary."

"But that would lessen over time—"

Julia stepped back and Daniel dropped his arms from her waist. "Look, aren't we supposed to be trying to find a killer?" she said, wiping a finger beneath her eyes. "Let's focus on that for now, shall we? What happened in Kendlewood this morning?"

"Julia, you were crying. You can't tell me you're willing just to let this go."

"You said you had a plan B?"

For a long moment, he held her eyes, second for second, strength for strength, before throwing his hands up in the air. "Fine. Have it your way."

She turned, dropped to her knees, and pulled out the blanket she had brought with her. She snapped it open and it softly fell to the sand. She then busied herself unloading the picnic basket. She laid out chicken mayonnaise sandwiches, apples, crisps, salad and ice-cold lemonade. She heard Daniel exhale heavily before he sat down beside her.

"This looks fantastic."

Julia was grateful he'd decided not to press her any further. Any more and she would break.

She passed him a paper plate. "Tuck in."

The next few minutes passed in silence as they ate.

Julia touched a napkin to her mouth. "So? Plan B?"

Daniel took a long drink before turning to face her, his eyes serious. "I need you to come with me to Kendlewood. I want you to have a look at these guys at the debt agencies just to satisfy myself that neither of them is the man you saw on the boat."

"OK," she said, slowly. "But what if it is one of them and he recognizes me? I don't mean to sound self-centered, but surely he'd come after me next?"

"The only other option is to pull them both in for an identity parade," he said. "But if we do that and one of them is the killer, they will know we're on to them. I'd prefer to execute a stakeout situation. I know it's a lot to ask."

Julia locked eyes with him. "I'll do it."

"He won't see you."

"I know." She swallowed. She trusted him and the thought wasn't half as scary as she'd expected it to be.

"I'm a detective, Julia. We'll keep you protected, I promise."

"We?"

"There will be other officers there. I ran the idea past my superior this morning and he's happy to go ahead as long as you understand the risks and sign a paper saying you are assisting us of your own free will."

The idea of going both thrilled and terrified her. "It's for Derek. I'll do it."

He gave a smile. "I never doubted you would."

****

Daniel glanced at Julia as they drove toward Kendlewood. She leaned forward in her seat, her hands clamped together in her lap. He knew she had to be anxious, but had every confidence that if one of these suspects was the killer, she'd identify him. With every passing hour he spent with her, Daniel was liking what he learned about the woman behind the gorgeous smile. Julia Kershaw was gutsy, determined and sexy as hell.

She turned and caught him staring.

"You okay?" he asked, quickly.

She sighed. "I will be once this is over."

"It's going to be fine. You'll do great."

"But what if I say it's not him and I'm wrong?" she asked, nervously. "I didn't get a good look at the killer's face. Even with my binoculars I couldn't see him properly."

He reached over and squeezed her hand. "Listen to me. What you saw at the beach will be stamped on your brain for a very long time."

"Cheer me up, why don't you?"

"Once Derek's killer fired that shot and you looked at him again, you would have automatically registered the way he was standing, the way he walked, moved..."

"Not necessarily."

"If Bainbridge is our man, I'm pretty sure you'll know."

"If I'm wrong you could be wasting time with him instead of tracking the real culprit."

"Julia, let me worry about that. You said he looked like he was full of himself and that describes Bainbridge perfectly."

Less than half an hour later, Daniel and Julia were watching Bainbridge through the plate glass window of Dial-A-Debt. Eliminating Lawson had been quick. Julia had dismissed him as the killer immediately. Lawson was too tall and too thin. Daniel had known from Julia's earlier description of the shooter it was unlikely to be Lawson but he wouldn't have been happy until she'd confirmed it.

Bainbridge was an entirely different matter.

Average height, immaculately groomed, vain—-all words Julia had used to describe the killer in her initial statement. The radio crackled to life.

"Suspect on the move, sir."

Daniel acknowledged the warning and looked up to see Bainbridge flick off the final light and plunge the office into darkness. Julia's breathing quickened beside him, but he didn't turn to look at her. Bainbridge had his back to them as he locked the door.

"Come on, come on, turn around," Julia muttered.

He did. Looking left and right up the street before he crossed the road, Bainbridge passed a safe distance from Daniel's unmarked car, enabling Julia to study him.

Julia released her breath in a rush. "Damn it."

"Well?" Daniel asked.

"It's not him. I'm sure of it. The man on the boat was...I don't know. Less balky, lighter in his movements and gestures."

"Like a woman?"

Julia smiled. "Well, I wouldn't say a woman. But he was a little feminine I suppose."

"Shit." Daniel slapped his hand against the steering wheel, his gaze stony as he looked straight ahead. Now what? It had been nearly a week and they had nothing. The total sum of a week long investigation was, he had Julia as the sole witness, Suzie acting as an informant, and Mrs. Palmer who had no clue what the victim, her husband, had been up to most of the time. "I was pinning my hopes on it being Bainbridge."

"Daniel?"

Blowing out a breath, he turned to face her. "Yeah?"

"You look as though you're ready to punch the windscreen out."

"Give me a minute." He picked up the radio and called off the assisting car. "Head back to the station, I'll be there shortly. Over."

He replaced the handset and curled his fingers back around the steering wheel. His mind raced through the miniscule amount of information he had to work on. A case always started with the victim. What had led to Derek Palmer being murdered in cold blood at a public beach? It made no sense.

"Why was Derek Palmer on that boat in the first place?" he muttered.

"What?"

"Why was Derek on the boat in the first place? He didn't strike me as the kind of guy who would take a leisurely boat trip on a Sunday afternoon."

"Well, no, but—"

"When we questioned Thelma about the boat, she said he often went fishing but never aboard a boat as big as you described. That's what bugging me, Julia. Why was he even there?"

"Maybe he was lured there? If Derek was frantic with worry over his mounting debt, he would have done anything if he thought it would clear it, wouldn't he?"

"You would think so. We need to find out *why* he was on that boat and then we'll find out *who* brought him there."

He gunned the engine and they both snapped on their seatbelts. Julia shifted back in her seat.

"Where are we going now?"

"You and I are going nowhere, *you* are going home."

"But_"

"I'll let you know if I need your help again."

He kept his eyes firmly fixed ahead and tried not to wince at the laser beam of pain her eyes were boring into his temple. God knows he'd love to spend more time with her and he'd do everything in his power to protect her, but she was at risk every time she was with him. He would rest a lot easier once he'd dropped her safely at home. Pulling into the traffic, he continued to ignore her glare.

"Are you working tonight?" he asked.

She folded her arms across her chest. "Yes."

Despite himself he fought the urge to smile. "Julia?"

"What?"

"Are you sulking?"

"No."

"Are you sure?"

"Go to hell."

He glanced across at her and laughed when she was unable to stop her mouth from curving into a smile.

"What are you laughing at?" she said. "You're the God damn dictator, not me."

He lifted his shoulders. "That's true, but in spite of that I still think you're bloody fantastic," he said.

"Yeah? Whereas I think you're a pain in the ass."

Grinning, he drove them back to Corkley Park and through the main High Street. But they were soon caught up in the work rush and found themselves sitting in a long queue of traffic. Daniel frowned when Julia hastily pushed herself further down into her seat.

He looked to the right and saw the bank. "Ah, I see. Marcus Lowell's the manager there, right? How can a guy like that manage a bank? It's insane."

"But no one knows what he's really like, do they? Hell, even I don't come to that."

"Fair enough."

"One thing's for sure I'd prefer to deal with a loan shark than have to walk in there and ask Marcus to lend me money."

"Don't even go there. If I had my way the man

would be locked up right now."

Rolling her eyes, she said, "Let's not start all that again. I've explained my reasons."

"Right. You don't want the hassle. It's still not good enough, Julia."

Her eyes turned icy cold. "Don't."

"I can't help it. Not until you've told me the real reason."

"You want the truth?" she asked angrily. "I'll tell you the truth. I stood in court and watched a judge rap my brother's killer on the knuckles and send him on his merry way. Now if you think my unwillingness to stand in court and face Marcus is cowardice, think what you like. You and I both know he'll be told not to be such a naughty boy next time and then the judge will slam down his gavel and send Marcus, bank manager extraordinaire, out the door."

Daniel opened his mouth to protest, then closed it again. What could he say? Her brother had been killed by one of his own. Her pain showed in the angry red patches staining her cheeks and the glassy shine in her eyes. He turned away, pursed his lips shut and moved along in line with the rest of the slow-moving traffic.

A little while later, they pulled to a stop in front of her house. He killed the engine.

"Julia?"

"What?"

Her tone was still frosty and Daniel drew in a long breath. "I understand what you're saying about Marcus—"

"No, Daniel, I don't think you do."

"Please, just let me finish."

Her face was still etched with anger but she offered a small nod and he took that as a sign to continue.

"Regardless of whether or not you trust the

system, I still think your decision not to even try to put that asshole behind bars, is the wrong one."

"Is that so?" she sniffed as she unsnapped her seatbelt and got out. She leaned down in the doorway. "Well, when I want or even care about your opinion, Inspector, I'll let you know."

Chapter Eight

Two days had passed and Julia had not seen Daniel since he'd dropped her off. After a second night of endless tossing and turning, she knew what he'd said was right. Twice she'd gotten out of bed and logged onto the Princess II website, and twice she'd typed her resignation and twice she'd deleted it.

With less than a week until she was due to leave, everything inside was pulling at her to stay. Her heart and principles were telling her she was needed here, not the other side of the world—but her head was telling her to get the hell out of here. She no longer had the physical and emotional strength to shoulder her mother's pain or deal with Marcus alone. The answer slammed violently into her chest just as it had again and again over the last forty-eight hours - maybe she didn't need to be alone anymore. Maybe Daniel was worth staying for.

But if she stayed in Corkley Park, the next six months would barely be easier than the six that had passed. She could not ignore the fact that Daniel's smile incessantly crept into her mind, sending her insides reeling. And yet she could not get involved with a cop and break what was left of her mother's heart.

She sat in the club's office, watching Jacob pour them both a drink. She loved him almost as much as her father, but it was time he accepted her leaving.

He handed her a stiff rum and coke and sat on the settee beside her. "So? What's all this about? I can't remember the last time you asked for a private chat like this. Just the two of us."

Julia took a deep breath. "I'm leaving in four days, Jacob. Why haven't you done anything about finding someone to replace me?"

He waved a hand dismissively. "I'll deal with it when it happens."

"But you know I've got a placement on that ship. It's a great opportunity. I *am* leaving."

He studied her for a long moment. "I get that, but what I want to know is *why are* you leaving?"

Julia took a sip of her drink. "Does it matter?"

He guffawed. "'Course it matters. Bloody hell, girl. You're running away. You know it and so do I."

"I am not running away, Jacob. Don't start with me."

"No? Why the sudden escape from Corkley then? You love this place, Julia. Always have, always will. There ain't no place of earth you'd rather be and that's the truth of it."

"Jacob, for God's sake. I'm never going to end up singing professionally if I stay in Corkley Park."

"Why don't you just settle down and have a family like a normal woman your age? That way, you won't have to bother yourself with such problems."

She saw the pout of his bottom lip and let out a fond laugh. "Ah, now we get to it. You don't want me to go."

He took a sip of his drink, carefully watching her over the rim of his glass. "I've heard rumors things are hotting up between you and that Inspector Conway. What do you have to say about that?"

She almost spat her mouthful of drink across the room.

"I say people should get their facts straight. Who's been saying things like that?" she demanded.

"Oooh, tetchy. Maybe there is some truth in it."

"Maybe it won't be so bad to get out of this town

for awhile," she said, defensively. "At least people won't be able to nose around in my business."

"Steady on, girl," Jacob grinned. "It's only a rumour."

She glared at him while trying to calm her breathing. "Nothing is going on between me and Inspector Conway," she said, evenly. "I'm leaving because I want to take this opportunity and sail with it. If you'll pardon the pun."

"You're not running away because of Derek's murder, are you?" he asked, narrowing his eyes. "'Cause if you are, you've got nothing to worry about on that score."

"I'm not running away because Derek was killed," she said, "But of course I've got something to worry about. I'm a witness."

"Doesn't matter."

Julia looked at him incredulously. "How can you say that? What if the killer comes after me, next?"

"He got his target. This guy had no interest in you."

Julia frowned. "You can't possibly know that, Jacob."

He shrugged. "It had nothing to do with you. Derek brought this on himself." He tipped his head back and finished his drink in one nonchalant gulp. "The bloke had it coming. He owed money left, right and center."

"I can't believe you're talking about him like this. Derek was your friend. So he got caught up in an evil addiction, and now you're saying he deserved to die?"

"All I'm saying is there's no reason for you to run away. Someone out there obviously had a problem with Derek. You shouldn't let it spook you."

Julia drained her own drink. "Just make sure you find my replacement soon. You know your customers expect live entertainment. The last thing you want to do is upset them."

"Everything will be fine. Stop worrying."

"And make sure you keep my leaving to yourself," said Julia. "It's important no one else knows."

Comprehension fell across his face. "Now we're getting to it. It's that damn bank manager."

Julia forced a smile. "Will you stop grasping at straws and say I can go and still have a job when I come back?" she teased in an attempt to distract him.

But he wasn't listening. "Is Lowell the reason you've got that cop stepping out with you? Is he protecting you from him?"

"I haven't seen Daniel for the last two days," said Julia, trying to look as though she couldn't care less. "He is not protecting me."

Jacob said nothing. Just silently stared at her. She struggled not to squirm beneath his gaze. "What?"

"I don't believe a word you've said. Half-truths, all of it." He stood and made for the door.

"Where are you going?"

"Downstairs to open the bar. You coming?"

"So that's it? You're going to sort out my replacement?"

He left the room. Julia lifted a hand to her head. The last thing she wanted was to leave town with bad feeling between her and Jacob. She loved him even if he was a stubborn old fool. She took a few deep breaths before hurrying down the spiral staircase and into the main bar. She sat on one of the stools and faced Jacob as he stood behind the bar.

"Jacob, come on. I don't want us falling out over this. I want to leave knowing everything is OK between us."

He met her eyes. "We're not going to fall out. I

love you, you know that. But I know this has
something to do with that bloody bank manager. Do
you know he's after one of your friends, now? The
jerk's going to get to you one way or another. "

Julia's stomach dropped to her shoes. She
gripped the bar. "What are you talking about?"

"That's what I thought our little chat was going
to be about," he said. "I thought you had finally come
to your senses and wanted me to sort the boy out."

"Jacob, what friend? What do you mean?"

"Suzie. He's seeing Suzie. You didn't know?" he
asked, fisting his hand on his hips. "That's old news,
kid. He took up with her as soon as you threw him
off."

"But that was weeks ago!" cried Julia. "Why
didn't Suzie tell me?"

He gestured toward the public phone at the end
of the bar. "Ring her. Ask her yourself."

Julia looked at the phone. "I can't believe she'd
go out with Marcus."

Jacob touched her arm, making her jump. "Why
don't you go see her? Get her to come to her senses?"

"I'll ask her to come into the club tonight," she
said, feeling shaky. *What was Marcus up to?*

"Good idea."

"I knew she wasn't herself the last time I saw
her. God knows that's what Marcus does best. He
affects the way you behave, the way you think..."

"And you're trying to tell me he has nothing to
do with you leaving? Pull the other one, kid, it's
written all over your face."

"Jacob—"

He held up a hand. "I don't want to talk about it
anymore. Make sure you look out for Suzie, she's got
a heart as soft as butter, that woman."

Julia looked at him. He was right. She could
deal with the likes of Marcus, but Suzie? Suzie
would remain faithful to the devil rather than upset

him. Julia walked to the phone and dialed Suzie's cell phone.

"No answer."

"Why don't you go see if you can track her down? You're not on until nine."

Julia glanced at her watch. "I want to go and check on Thelma too, so I'll drop by Suzie's house on the way."

"Why are you going to see Thelma again?"

She looked at him in disbelief. "Because her husband of forty years was killed less than a week ago. What's wrong with you, Jacob?"

"Nothing."

Julia snatched her bag from the bar. "I'd take a good long look at yourself if I were you. Derek was your friend."

"Derek Palmer was a selfish asshole come the end."

Julia threw her hands up in the air. "I'm not listening to any more of this. I'm going to find Suzie, and I don't want to hear you mutter another bad word about Derek while I'm around, OK?"

Jacob puffed up his chest. "You need to remember who the boss is around here."

"Yeah? Well, you won't be my boss for much longer, will you?"

She turned on her heel and marched out of the club, ignoring Jacob's explicit cursing behind her.

****

Julia took the steps two at a time, then rang the doorbell to Suzie's apartment. No answer. She crouched down and called through the letterbox. "Suze? Are you in there? It's Julia."

Still no answer. The apartment was devoid of the usual thump, thump, thump of some forgotten 1980s pop band. Julia pulled her cell from her bag and dialed Suzie's number, but it kicked straight to answer phone.

"Hi, Suzie, it's me. Can you call me back as soon as possible? It's important."

She snapped the phone shut, walked back down the steps and got into her car. She'd go and see Thelma and hope Suzie rang while she was there.

Twenty minutes later, Julia was watching Thelma as she made tea and carefully placed some home-baked blueberry muffins on a plate. It was nearing seven o'clock in the evening and Thelma thought it perfectly normal to be serving afternoon tea.

"How are you, Thelma?" she asked gently, taking the tray from the older woman's hands.

"Oh, not too bad, dear."

"Are you eating?"

She laughed softly. "Of course. Don't you waste your time worrying about me. I'd much prefer you tried to find out what Inspector Conway is doing about finding out who killed my Derek."

Julia raised her eyebrows. "I'd assumed Daniel, I mean Inspector Conway, would have at least called to tell you about what happened in Kendlewood. Didn't he do that?"

"You mean the debt agencies?" Thelma asked.

"Yes, did he tell you I went with them to try to identify one of them as the man who shot Derek?"

"Inspector Conway came around and sat with me for most of Saturday evening." Thelma sighed. "Such a pleasant man. I got the distinct feeling he didn't want to be alone anymore than I did. Do you think he's lonely, too, dear?"

Julia turned away. "I've no idea, Thelma. Anyway, you should be more concerned about yourself than Inspector Conway."

Julia felt Thelma's gaze on her for a moment longer before she proceeded to fill two cups from the teapot. "That was two days ago," Thelma continued. "And I've not heard a peep from the police since.

Have you, dear?"

"No, but then again, the police are not obliged to tell me anything if they don't want to."

Thelma looked at her with eyes suddenly shining with unshed tears. "Even if you're a witness? And a friend? Derek loved you just as I do. Why would they keep things from you?"

"Because I'm still a member of the public, Thelma," Julia said, gently. "I'm doing all I can to help Inspector Conway and he has involved me to a point."

"But there's got to be more we can do."

Julia closed her eyes to the wretched helplessness etched on Thelma's face. What would happen after she left town? Would Daniel continue to keep Thelma informed of what was going on? Could she trust the police to do the right thing? But as she opened her eyes, Julia knew she couldn't. Phil's death was still so raw and she had to face facts that since Daniel had left after their argument over Marcus, he'd obviously decided he no longer needed her help.

"Julia?"

"Mmmm?"

"Isn't there anything we can do?"

Julia chewed at her bottom lip as she met Thelma's scared eyes. She had to do something. She felt a twist deep in her belly as an idea struck her. She put down her cup and slowly smiled. "There's nothing Inspector Conway can do to stop me doing a little investigating of my own, is there?"

Thelma's eyes widened. "Oh, no, dear. I wasn't asking you—"

Julia edged forward on her seat. "It's all right. Trust me, Thelma. Everything will be fine."

"But what are you going to do?"

"I need you to think really hard. Maybe there's something you know but didn't think important when you spoke to Daniel."

Confusion creased Thelma's brow. "Like what? I've told him everything I know."

Excitement rippled along Julia's nerve endings as she took Thelma's hands in her own. "You said Derek was in debt and had a gambling problem. But what about Derek himself? Tell me more about *him*, the person. Not the one I knew, not the friendly shop keeper everyone loved, but the man he was behind closed doors. Maybe something you thought irrelevant will be just what leads the police to finding his killer."

"But Derek's life was the store. That was Derek in a nutshell. He didn't have any hobbies apart from fishing, which I've already told you about. There's nothing else I can tell you."

"What about his friends? Did you know any of them?"

"Not really. We used to go dancing with a few of our friends from time to time, but Derek lost interest in doing that months ago. Any other friends he had, he kept to himself." She pulled a hand from Julia's to wipe away a stray tear. "But then, I never showed any interest in getting to know them, either. I was quite happy to sit here, in front of the TV without him chattering all the way through the Antiques Roadshow. Why did I do that? Why did I waste so much precious time watching TV?"

Julia got up from the armchair and joined Thelma on the settee. She stole an arm around the older woman's bony shoulder. "Don't go upsetting yourself, Thelma."

"But there's nothing else I can tell you, dear." Thelma sniffed. "God knows I haven't slept much since I lost him and I still haven't thought of anything that will help."

Julia stared at a spot on the carpet, her mind working overtime. "You may have already thought of something that might help."

"I have?"

Julia gave her an excited squeeze. "The store. Has anyone gone over the store with a fine tooth comb?"

"I think so."

"But you're not sure?"

"No. Yes. I'm sure the police have. Why? Do you think they might have missed something?"

"It's possible. Why don't you give me the keys and I'll head over there first thing in the morning?" asked Julia. "I'd go tonight but I have to work and I don't fancy looking around the store on my own after dark."

"But surely you're not thinking of doing this alone? You need to ring Inspector Conway. He'll know what to do."

Julia felt her cheeks heat. "I'll be fine. There's no need to bother him."

Thelma narrowed her eyes. "What's going on? He's a good, kind and intelligent man. Why wouldn't you want him there? Please tell me your mother hasn't passed her distorted views about the police onto you," she said. "Because she's wrong, sweetie. Heartbroken but wrong."

Julia found it hard to meet Thelma's eyes. "Of course she hasn't. I just think it would be easier if I had a look around the store by myself. There's no point in taking up valuable police time if there's nothing there."

But Thelma shook her head. "Your brother was killed in a tragic case of mistaken identity. You can not carry around this hatred of the police. You may need them one day. Ring the Inspector," Thelma insisted.

"OK." Thelma touched a finger to Julia's chin and she had no choice but to meet her eyes. "Thelma, I know what I'm doing- -"

"Are you falling for him?" Thelma asked, softly. "Is that it?"

Julia laughed. "Don't be silly."

"You can't fool me, my girl. I've known you since you were a child."

Julia looked away. "He's nice, Thelma...and professional. That's all."

"So why not take him with you to the store if he's so *professional*?" she said with a faint smile.

Julia stood and hitched her bag onto her shoulder. "Why don't you stop sniffing for scandal and give me the keys instead."

Sighing deeply, Thelma pushed herself to her feet. "Wait there. You're as stubborn as your father, do you know that?"

Julia grinned. "Yep."

****

Julia tugged at the hem of her skirt, which seemed to be getting suspiciously shorter with each performance. Jacob always insisted she packed the club with her talent--and as far as she was concerned, her 'talent' didn't include her legs. At least the clothes she'd be wearing aboard the Princess II were more tasteful. The manager had told her it would be floor-length gowns and professional make-up all the way. It pleased her to think she would soon see the back of thigh-high boots and miniscule skirts.

The band struck up the opening bars of 'A Natural Woman' and Julia stepped onto the stage. As she looked out into the crowd, she saw the ratio of men by far outweighed the women, and was greeted by a barrage of whooping and wolf-whistling. She forced a smile and tried not to acknowledge that half the audience had known her since she was in knee-high socks.

Julia was in no mood to entertain tonight but she owed it to Jacob to do the best job possible until

149

she left. She took a breath and began to sing. Just as she was coming to the half way mark of her set, she spotted two familiar figures walking through the swinging doors of the bar.

Her heart leapt into her throat and her hand turned clammy around the microphone. How could he? How could *she*? Marcus led Suzie to one of the cozy booths that lined each side of the room. Nausea lurched in Julia's stomach. She could barely stand to watch Marcus lean in close to Suzie's ear before he turned and headed for the bar. Julia noted the tension in Suzie's face. Who could ignore the way her hands were folded tightly together in her lap, or the way her eyes darted nervously around the room?

Somehow Julia managed to finish her song before signaling to the lead guitarist she wanted to take the halfway break now instead of after the next track. She bowed to rapturous applause before she exited the stage and headed straight for Suzie.

"What do you think you're doing?" Julia all but demanded, sliding into the seat beside her friend. "Weren't you listening when I told you what Marcus is like?"

"Don't spoil this for me, Julia. Please."

"Spoil it for you? What are you talking about? I'm trying to help you."

Suzie pulled a packet of cigarettes from her bag. "I don't need your help. What I need is some male company. I've been warming my own bed sheets for far too long."

The image of Marcus touching her friend was more than Julia could stomach. She snatched the cigarette from Suzie's mouth. "You have to stop this right now. You deserve better than some psycho who's going to start following you around, demanding to know where you are twenty-four hours a day and then——when you eventually come to your senses—refusing to let you break things off."

"Marcus is not like that," said Suzie, snatching the cigarette out of Julia's hand and quickly lighting it.

"So you think I'm lying?" asked Julia, incredulously.

"Yes."

Julia thrust her wrist in front of Suzie's face. "There. How's that for lying?"

Julia watched her friend swallow as her eyes lingered at the yellow bruising. She shrugged. "What is that supposed to prove?"

"For God's sake, Suze, Marcus grabbed me and dragged me across my own bloody living room trying to make me listen to him. The man's not right."

"It still doesn't mean he'd do it to me."

"Can you hear what you're saying? Have you asked yourself why he's suddenly so interested in you?"

Suzie exhaled a slow stream of smoke. "Oh, that's just great. You think he's too good-looking for the likes of me? Thanks a lot, Julia."

"Am I interrupting something, ladies?"

The hairs on the back of Julia's neck stood to attention at the sound of his voice. Reluctantly, she lifted her eyes to face Marcus. His gaze locked on hers, cold and unyielding. She forced a smile.

"Not at all."

"Good, good."

"Of course, you already know Suzie and I are good friends, don't you?" Julia asked.

He slid into the seat opposite them and pushed a glass of white wine toward Suzie. "Of course I do. In fact, this is more awkward than I thought it would be."

Julia arched an eyebrow. "Awkward?"

"When Suzie suggested we come here for a drink, I was concerned what your reaction would be to seeing the two of us together, but Suzie insisted you wouldn't mind at all."

"I don't," said Julia through clenched teeth.

He smiled. "Really? I was watching you scold Suzie from the bar. There can only be two reasons why one woman would speak to another with such venom. Either you're jealous of her shoes or her man. Which is it, Julia?"

"You and I both know you're with Suzie because of me, Marcus. Just admit it so Suzie can see what you're really like."

He laughed, the sound icy cold. "Do you hear that, my love?" he said, reaching for Suzie's hand but his eyes not leaving Julia's. "I must say Julia isn't the good friend to you I thought she was."

Ignoring him, Julia snapped her head round to look at Suzie. "Suzie, please."

For a long moment, her friend met her eyes and Julia thought she was going to see sense but then Suzie shook her head. "No, Julia. We've been going out for nearly two months now and we love each other—"

"Two months? You love each other? Have you lost your mind?"

Suzie glared at her. "Yes, I love him. That's why I haven't told you. Marcus said you wouldn't be happy for us."

Julia inhaled a long breath before slowly releasing it. "I can't believe you're being this naïve, Suze." She turned on Marcus. "What have you done to her?"

He grinned. "Me? The fact that your friend is happy and in love is something to be angry about? I really do not understand you, Julia."

She leaned forward. "If you two are so in love, why were you around my house just a few days ago? Letting yourself in, creeping around like—"

"I was not in your house," Marcus interrupted, reaching for Suzie's hand. "Don't start making up stories in a bid to split Suzie and I apart. It will never work."

"I don't need to make up stories, Marcus. Suzie will believe me over you any day, won't you Suze?" she asked, turning to her friend.

Indecision shone clear in Suzie's eyes and Julia waited for her answer with her heart thudding hard against her chest. "Suze?"

But then Suzie squeezed Marcus' hand. "No, Julia. I'm not going to let you do this. I love Marcus and I'd do anything for him. Can you just leave us alone now if you can't be happy for us?"

Julia looked from Suzie's turned cheek to Marcus' wolverine smile. She shook her head. "I don't know where the hell you're going with this, Marcus but it absolutely stinks."

"Why don't you just concentrate on the handsome Inspector Conway and leave us alone, Julia? Where is he tonight by the way?" he asked, looking around the bar. "I would have imagined him sitting at the bar watching you perform. Waiting patiently to walk you home."

Julia stood, but as she turned to walk away, Marcus grabbed her wrist, making her wince. "How *is* the investigation of poor Derek Palmer's death going by the way?"

She snatched her hand from his grip. "Why would *you* care?"

He shrugged. "I am always interested in the community, Julia. You forget I am quite the figure head of Corkley Park."

She huffed. "I don't think so, Marcus. And don't ever lay a hand on me again. Got it?"

And with that Julia turned and marched away.

Chapter Nine

At ten thirty the following morning, Julia stood outside Derek's store, staring numbly at the huge front window now plastered with newspaper. Thelma had arranged for the window to be covered so no one could peer in and speculate on her husband's secret life. Although details of Derek's gambling hadn't been released, details of his murder had, so gawkers as well as genuine sympathetic well-wishers now passed the store on a daily basis.

She took a steadying breath, stepped forward and slipped the key into the lock. The bell above the door announced her arrival. Julia softly closed, then locked the door behind her. She took a moment to look around. Sunlight filtered through gaps in the paper, cascading sunbeams across the tiled floor and illuminating the dust motes that danced in the musty air.

Derek's Den was an old-fashioned store, like those portrayed in black and white movies. You could buy everything here—from a quarter of sugared almonds to seedlings for your garden. Julia smiled fondly as she recalled how from her first visit in a stroller with her mother to her last visit a few weeks ago, Derek had always greeted her with a beaming smile and peppermint lollipop. Tears threatened to spill so she quickly walked through to the back office and flicked on the light.

Organized chaos claimed Derek's office. The only way Julia could tell it hadn't been ransacked was by the array of colored post-it notes stuck to various files, papers and stock. Thelma was right—Derek had been more than a little distracted toward the end of his life.

She closed the door and took a seat behind his desk. But when she stretched out her legs, her foot knocked up against something hidden in the kneehole. Leaning down, Julia picked up the aluminum baseball bat and laid it across her knees. *You were scared, Derek, really scared. Never in a million years would you have considered using this unless you were in serious trouble.* She put down the bat and tugged on one of the four desk drawers. It rolled open.

She pulled out a leather-bound book and opened it. A ledger. Maybe there would be something in here that would give some clue as to whom Derek had owed money, or at least the amounts he was paying. She placed the book on the desk and flicked through the pages.

Half an hour later, her eyes swam with figures but she hadn't found anything useful. She closed the book, and reached inside the second drawer. Among the various pens, pencil and cigarette packets, she found a diary. Frowning, she turned to the date when Derek had been killed and worked backward.

He had been shot on the 30th of July, a date Julia knew she'd never forget. The space was empty. Nothing. Not as much as a delivery due. She continued to turn the pages. She was beginning to think her idea to come to the store would be a fruitless one, when she noticed a tiny asterisk marked in the corner of every other Thursday.

Payment day, maybe? Her heart picked up speed. It had to be. Or it had to be at least something to do with his debts or the money laundering racket he'd gotten himself involved with. Everything to do with the store was outlined in plain black and white—deliveries were marked, stock takes, even cleaning days. This meant something else.

A rush of adrenaline sped through her and Julia stuffed the diary under her arm and got to her feet. She'd go and see Thelma. Maybe she'd have some idea what the asterisk could mean, but if not...

Just as she moved toward the door, the bell above the shop door tinkled. Julia froze. Had she forgotten to lock the front door? She didn't think so, so she grabbed the baseball bat and hurried to a closed closet door. She climbed in among the brooms, mops and buckets and held her breath as she heard the office door open.

Julia strained to listen. Whoever was in the office, was slowly making their way around the room. From the sound of the footsteps they were walking around in a circle. She gripped the bat handle harder, trying to focus above the noise of the blood thumping in her ears.

The footsteps came to a halt outside the closet door.

"How long are you planning on staying in there?" he asked. "I know it's a mess in here but it's got to be better than standing in the closet."

Julia fought a smile. Daniel. Thank God. Tilting her chin, she opened the door and came face to face with him.

Her heart shot straight into her throat. That damn sexy smile of his should be deemed illegal.

"What are *you* doing here?" she demanded.

"Is that any way to greet your local Detective Inspector?"

"Yeah, well, you shouldn't be creeping—"

As she stepped forward, her foot got tangled between the baseball bat and a plastic bucket. The next thing she knew, she was sprawling forward into Daniel's arms as the bat and bucket clattered to the floor.

"Whoa, are you all right?" he asked, gripping her

waist.

She could tell by his tone he was trying his hardest not to laugh.

"I'm fine."

She let go of his biceps but he didn't take his hands from her waist. There was barely enough space between them for the air to revolve. She could feel his body heat. Sending up a silent prayer that he would not enjoy this moment too much, she lifted her head.

"Go on then, get it over with."

"What?"

"Say what you need to say. Laugh if you want. Just get it over and done with."

"Laughing is the last thing I want to do."

She met his gaze, and was trapped. He brought his lips down hard on hers. Her arms slipped back to those beautiful biceps and she dug her fingernails into the hard muscle.

"Julia."

He whispered her name against the smooth curve of her neck, sending tremors of desire coursing through her. She wanted his hands everywhere. Wanted him to discover her while she explored every inch of him. Had wanted this since she'd burst into his office.

And that was the thought that sent her reeling back to reality.

"Stop." She pushed at his arms. "Daniel, stop."

He pulled away from her, his eyes fiery with arousal, his hands slightly trembling as he lifted them to his hair. "I want you, Julia."

"Are you crazy?" She turned her back to him so he couldn't see her own yearning reflected in her eyes. "This is madness. I'm leaving town. You're a cop—"

"I know, and if you think this is wrong, unethical, that's nothing compared to the battle I've

157

been fighting with myself. But there's nothing I can do about it. I've never been as attracted to another woman as I am to you."

The admission made her want to smile but she quickly trapped her bottom lip between her teeth. She could not enjoy this moment, she had to quash it. Her brother's face flashed in front of her closed eyes like a cruel reminder of how weak she was not to fight this temptation.

She spun around. "I can never be with you. Why don't you understand that?"

He squeezed his own eyes tightly shut, before opening them again. "What happened to your brother was not my fault."

"Maybe not, but I know what you're capable of. I've seen it with my own eyes."

"What I'm *capable* of? What is it you think you've seen?"

"Cops kill."

"Julia, come on—-"

He stepped toward her but she held up a hand. "Don't," she said, her voice cracking.

He ignored her, reached out and gently pulled her back into his arms. Hot tears pricked her eyes and she inhaled his scent like oxygen. When the smell hit her brain, her heart—she had no way of stopping herself from burying her face in his shirt and letting the tears fall.

He said nothing, just held her. She had no idea how long they stood together like that, but when he shifted and moved away from her, she immediately felt cold.

He brushed his thumbs beneath her eyes. "We could make this work, you know."

She shook her head and her shoulders slumped. "No. No, we couldn't."

"I meant what I said before. I want you, and maybe you're going to need some convincing. But that's fine. Even if it takes me ten years, I'll do it."

"Daniel—"

"Tonight is your night off and you're going to spend it with me." She opened her mouth to protest but he held up a finger. "No arguments. Just come to the Cove." He paused. "Please, Julia. Now that I've found you, I'm not letting you go without a damn good fight."

"You're not listening to me—"

"I am, but I'm confident I can change your mind," he said with a smile that set her whole body tingling. "Come on, take a risk. I dare you."

She crossed her arms. "You won't change my mind. It doesn't matter how I feel about you. I cannot put my mother through that."

"Through what? Surely she wants to see you happy?"

It suddenly occurred to Julia that she had no idea whether or not that was true. "I would be sleeping with the enemy, Daniel."

He smiled. "Sleeping with?"

The tone of his voice should have been cocky, but to Julia it sounded sexy. Keeping her eyes fixed to his, she ignored the erotic pull deep down in her stomach and instead, poked a finger to his chest. "This is not a joke."

"Believe me, thinking of sleeping with you does not make me laugh."

"Daniel—"

"The Cove? Tonight?"

She looked at him for a long, long moment. "Fine, I'll go with you."

He lifted her finger and pressed a kiss to its tip. "Good."

Several seconds ticked by before Julia managed to drag her attention away from his lips. Finally, she cleared her throat and carefully extracted her hand from his grasp.

"Don't you think we should be focusing on Derek's murder and not us?" She paused. "What are you doing here, anyway?"

"Thelma rang me this morning and said you were going to be here."

"I told her I didn't want to involve you."

"Yes, she said as much when I stopped by for a key."

"Why would she...?"

"She knows there's a killer out there who went after Derek for a reason. She also knows it's dangerous to come here alone when that killer could come back at any time to collect what's owed him."

The significance of what he was saying made Julia feel queasy. She blew out a breath. "You're right. Of course, you're right. I should have called you."

"I'm here now," he said before turning and rifling through a stack of papers on Derek's desk. "Did you come here looking for something in particular? Because my team has already been through the place and found nothing useful."

"I know."

"But you thought you'd double check anyway?" he asked, as the corners of his mouth twitched. "There's nothing here. Unless, of course, you know something I don't?"

Julia realized she'd left the diary in the closet. "Just a second."

She walked back to the closet, retrieved the book, and held it out to Daniel. "I found something interesting in here. If you look, you'll see there is an asterisk marked on every other Thursday. It's not much but it might be significant."

"Mmmm," Daniel scored a finger down the pages. "It could. But it's not enough to give us any headway. We'll speak to Thelma about it."

"It won't hurt to take another look around, will

it?"

"I suppose not and after all you knew Derek. I didn't. Maybe there will be something here that looks out of place to you."

With a curt nod Julia walked to a bureau and looked through the various invoices, envelopes and letters pushed into the cubby holes. She spoke over her shoulder.

"Did you manage to locate the boat?"

"Mmm?"

Julia smiled. He was already re-engrossed in his work. "Nothing. It's not important."

"I've got a team following up a lead about the boat right now. There are one or two that sound close to your description down at the harbor. I'm hoping to get a call this side of lunch time."

"Any more theories why Derek was on the boat in the first place? I can only guess a meeting was set up and he was basically walking to his death. The killer had every intention of shooting him. I'm sure of it. No one is that cool, that calm, unless they are mentally prepared for it."

She heard Daniel exhale a frustrated breath and turned to face him. "You okay?"

He ran a hand over his face. "I agree with you. Derek's death was arranged and carried out on a pre-mediated plan. We need to locate that boat and the loan sharks. I've been around enough to know that businessmen like those Derek was involved with often get someone else to do their dirty work."

Julia tapped the letter she was holding against her chin. "In what way?"

"My gut tells me we're looking for a third person. A hired assassin of some sort. Whoever killed Derek was not necessarily the person who wanted him dead."

"You think the shooter was working for someone else? God, that's awful."

"It makes the whole case more difficult to solve. If the guy on the boat was an assassin, they are trained to disappear."

Julia studied the tension in his shoulders and the firm clench of his jaw. "But you'll find him, won't you?"

"My father's assassin was never found. Maybe Derek's killer will be my first escapee. My first failure as a cop."

Julia stared at him. "Your father was assassinated? When you told me about hiding in the cupboard, I assumed—"

"My father was an undercover cop, Julia. A cop who worked hard and risked his life day after day to catch the bad guys. He was running with a gang of underground drug traffickers and someone from the neighborhood snitched on him."

"Daniel, I..." She let her words hang in the air and stepped toward him, but he held up a hand.

"It's done and I've accepted that it's a huge possibility his killer will never serve a day behind bars, but if I don't find Derek's killer?" He paused and when he looked at her, Julia's breath caught in her throat to see the rage there. "I will have failed as a cop *and* a son."

"You cannot think like that, Daniel. Your father is looking down on you now and he's proud. Really proud."

He didn't answer her, but turned back to Derek's desk. As she watched him bend over the papers in front of him, Julia fought the despair that threatened to crawl its way inside of her. She couldn't believe that just two weeks ago, she had been looking forward to escaping her mother's endless sorrow and Marcus' frightening volatility. Now all she wanted was to spend every passing second with this man she hadn't even known then.

She glanced at the letter—or what she'd thought

was a letter—in her hand and all thoughts of her and Daniel vanished. It was a piece of stationery, not a letter. Blocks of figures had been scribbled onto the paper, dates strewn in the margin and initials haphazardly marked over the page.

But it wasn't the information that had her getting up from her seat, it was the creamy, heavy bonded texture of the paper. She'd seen paper like this before, held it, but where?

It definitely hadn't been in Derek's store.

She pushed it onto the desk in front of Daniel.

"I recognize this stationery," she said, urgently. "I've seen it before."

He picked up the paper, and scanned the scribblings. "You recognize it? From where?"

"I don't know. That's the problem. But it doesn't fit in with this store."

****

Daniel gunned the engine and headed toward Julia's house. She hadn't been too happy with him once he'd reverted back to cop mode after she'd found that sheet of familiar paper. But he hadn't been able to help himself. It had given him something solid to hunt down when his hope of solving this case had been fading fast. He'd left rather abruptly, he knew, but it was either that or spend the afternoon searching for other fruitless leads, and risk losing what little faith Julia already had in him to bring Derek's killer to justice.

He soon discovered she wasn't at home nor at the club. He'd tried her cell but it was either switched off or she was ignoring him. No doubt that meant their date for tonight was off. His cop demeanor tended to have a mood-dampening effect on her, and part of him couldn't blame her for it.

But a cop was what he was, and a cop was what he would stay. He made his way into town and walked into a coffee shop for some much needed caffeine. He placed his order with the young girl serving, then turned his back to the counter.

And saw Julia. Relief swept through him and warmed his blood. She sat by the window, the sunlight dancing off her blonde hair as she read a paperback novel. Daniel smiled. Never had he seen anyone so oblivious to their own beauty. He looked left and right and was quick to spot at least three guys, surreptitiously checking her out.

Back off, boys. She's mine.

Daniel tipped the girl behind the counter, took his coffee and approached Julia's table. He cast a shadow across the pages of her book and she looked up. Her spontaneous smile diminished the second her eyes met his.

"Oh, it's you," she said, giving an inelegant sniff.

Daniel fought the pull at the corners of his mouth. She was fabulous when she was annoyed. "Yes, unfortunately it's me. May I join you?" Without waiting for an answer, he pulled up a chair and straddled it. "I wanted to check what time you want me to pick you up tonight."

"I don't think so, Daniel. It wouldn't be wise."

So they were back to that, again. "I want to spend some time with you on my night off, Julia. What wrong with that?"

She didn't answer.

"Come on, Julia," he said. "Come to the beach with me tonight. I'm a great outdoor cook."

"Why should I?"

He arched a hopeful eyebrow. "Because I'm begging?"

She lifted her eyes to the ceiling for a few seconds as though considering his plea before looking him straight in the eyes. Daniel's heart kicked hard against his chest. Her eyes sparkled like emeralds.

"On one condition."

"Anything."

"You bring plenty of chicken drumsticks thickly marinated in honey and mustard," she said, her tongue flicking out to moisten her lips. "And for dessert, I want strawberries and cream. Oh, and not that horrible, low-fat stuff either. I want cream so thick it has to be spooned on, not poured."

As well as feeling like a teenager who had managed to secure a date with the hottest girl in school, Daniel found the whole tongue thing immensely erotic. He cleared his throat. "Deal. Eight o'clock," he said, getting up from his chair. "On the dot." He turned to walk away, then suddenly remembered something. "Oh, and Julia? Bring a bikini."

He smiled as she started sputtering behind him.

Chapter Ten

Julia opened the door to find Daniel holding a huge bouquet of yellow roses.

"An apology for annoying you earlier today."

Damn him. "They're beautiful, Daniel, thank you. Come in."

Turning, she headed for the kitchen, leaving him, to close the door. There was no use in denying that the flowers had just quashed her final scrap of indecision as to whether or not she would actually step outside the door with him. The bikini she'd put on under her clothes was merely a precaution.

She filled the biggest vase she had with water, while willing her heartbeat to slow down. She'd had all afternoon to prepare herself for this, to prepare for *him*, but was suddenly, incredibly, inexplicably nervous. And when he spoke softly against her ear, her heart leapt into her throat.

"You look lovely."

Heat covered her body in one quickly laid blanket. She squeezed her eyes shut and her thighs together. Electricity crackled dangerously between them. She swallowed. "Thanks."

When she moved, he stepped back and she walked to the small kitchen table and placed the roses in the center.

"They're stunning. You shouldn't have."

When no response came, she turned to look at him.

"Daniel?"

He didn't meet her eyes. Instead, his gaze lazily appreciated every inch of her body, making her feel naked and exposed. She inhaled a shaky breath. It felt good and bad, all at the same time.

"We'd better get going," she heard herself say, taking a step past him. "It will be dark before long." Before she could change her mind again, she hurried into the hallway, grabbed her handbag from the bottom of the banister, and stepped out the front door.

Enjoying the light pressure of his hand at the small of her back, Julia walked to the car and decided that whatever her mother's feelings toward cops were, tonight they would have to be pushed to the back of her mind. After all, this was possibly the last time she would see Daniel Conway for a few months.

And despite her bravado, Julia wanted the last night with him to matter.

The short drive to the beach passed in silence. Julia snuck a few furtive glances at his handsome profile and was sure Daniel stole a few, too. Now, as she leaned her elbows back into the sand and looked around her, she felt the tension seep from her shoulders. With darkness settling softly around them, Julia watched him from the corner of her eye as he popped the cork on a bottle of champagne and filled two glasses.

He held one out to her. "Enjoy."

"What shall we drink to?" she asked.

"To us."

He touched his glass to hers and drank. She followed suit. The velvety liquid exploded against her tongue and she savored its rich golden taste.

"So," Daniel began, "Are you hungry? Or do you want to swim first?"

She eyed him over the rim of her glass. "You open champagne, then decide you want to swim? No way, Mister. We can't let champagne this good turn warm, it will be ruined."

"Fear not young lady, for I have thought of everything."

Julia bit back a smile as he wiggled his eyebrows. He turned to his holdall and produced a wine bucket, then dug into the cooler and filled it with huge chunks of ice.

She nodded her approval. "I'm impressed."

"Good. Now strip."

"Daniel!"

But coyness didn't suit her, and when Daniel stripped off to reveal his swimming shorts beneath, Julia laughed and removed her own clothes to show that she, too, had come prepared. Daniel let out a low whistle, and Julia felt her insides quiver but secretly hoped she hadn't gone too far.

She put her hands on her hips, smiling mischievously. "Did I do something I shouldn't have?"

He gestured with his finger, pointing up and down her bikini-clad body. "That's...that's..."

"Goodness, me, Detective Inspector, are you all right?"

"But...but there's nothing to it!" he sputtered.

She looked down at her body in mock surprise. "This
old thing? Don't be silly—I'd wear this swimming with my mom."

She left him standing there open-mouthed and sprinted toward the water, wearing a huge grin. But he was too fast and when he grabbed her by the waist, Julia didn't know whether to cry out in surprise or scream with delight. He carried her into the water and when the cool waves touched her bare skin, she clung to his body heat.

When she'd stopped laughing enough to look into his eyes, what she saw there sent tremors through every part of her body. His eyes reflected everything she was feeling. Emotions swirled and battled in their depths—lust, need, laughter, joy...love. Julia's heart soared.

They spoke at the same time.

"Daniel, I—"

"Julia, there's something you should know," he said, as he held her firmly in his arms.

The sounds of the water lulled, the waves hushed and the birds circling overhead flew silently away. His gaze wandered over her face.

"I'm falling in love with you."

The shock of him saying it out loud robbed her of speech. Instead, she kissed him and knew that this was it. His admission, said so easily, so simply had just made what she was feeling, what was happening between them real. The salty taste of him slid over her lips and her hands automatically lifted to hold his strong jaw. Her heart beat hard beneath her ribcage, her body hummed with the need for him.

How long they kissed, Julia had no idea, but knew she had never felt such joy, such heartbreak— or faced such a difficult decision.

He loved her.

And she loved him. She shivered. Suddenly out here just the two of them alone in the ocean, Julia could feel her brother looking down on her. But she didn't feel his anger or disappointment, all she felt with astonishing clarity was his permission. She could feel it seeping through her skin, deeper and deeper into her heart.

She held the moment, strained to hear him against the pure joy of being in Daniel's arms, feeling his body pressed so tightly to her own. Or maybe she was imagining Phil's approval so she could continue this journey with Daniel guilt-free?

She pressed her lips harder to Daniel's, sought his tongue with hers and clung her legs a little tighter around his waist—and prayed Phil would fight through the conflicting fears and hopes battling through her mind until she could hear him telling her exactly what she should do.

Only once their skin had started to wrinkle did they walk hand in hand from the water. Collapsing onto the blanket, Julia looked at the black, velvety sky above them. Night had fallen without her noticing. She turned her head, watched Daniel's chest fall and rise beside her and wondered what was supposed to happen next. It seemed Phil had left her to find her own way.

Her gaze wandered up his body to his face—and felt her cheeks heat to catch him watching her.

"So, do I get to seduce you now or after we've eaten?" he asked, quietly.

Her mouth twitched. "Who says you get to do that either way?"

She sat up and reached for her glass of champagne from the cooler. But before it touched her lips, Daniel had taken it from her hand and put it back.

He smiled and her heart turned over. *Damn him and that sexy smile.* Her mind raced, her heart jumped, but she did absolutely nothing to stop him. He leaned over her and his lips touched hers. She closed her eyes and breathed in his exquisite masculine scent as he brushed his fingers down the side of her face, her neck, her collar bone. She pressed her lips firmly against his, her tongue pushing hungrily into his mouth. She wanted him. Oh, God, she wanted him.

Leaning back until she lay flat against the blanket, Julia drew him down with her. His chest pressed hard against her breasts, his torso flat against hers. And when he inched her legs apart to place one muscular leg there, Julia's breathing quickened.

"Do you really want this?" he asked, looking

deep into her eyes.

"Of course I do."

"I was only teasing about the seduction, but now I'm serious. More serious than I've ever been in my life." He paused, his gaze dropping to her lips before meeting her eyes once more. "But if you want me to stop..."

He let the sentence hang in the air. She lifted a hand to brush the hair that had fallen into his eyes.

"If you stop now, I may have to seriously hurt you."

Grinning, he took her hand and pressed a kiss to its palm. "God, you're fantastic."

Feeling gloriously sexy, Julia stretched her arms above her head knowing right now this was exactly what they should be doing. Whatever happened between them from here on in, she wanted Daniel to make love to her, wanted to feel him deep inside of her even if she could only experience it this one precious time. She sighed happily as he nibbled at the tender skin at her shoulder before making a tantalizing path toward her breast.

But when he inched back the wet bra of her bikini, the game became intense and her smile slowly slipped. He replaced the cool night air that nipped at her breast with the warmth of his breath and the heat of his tongue. She sucked in a breath as he skillfully sent waves of sensation coursing through her body.

His leg lifted urgently against the material between her legs and she lustfully returned the pressure. Dropping her hands, she scored her nails through his hair, across his shoulders and down his muscular back, savoring the rush of his breath against her nipple.

She reached for him and pushed him gently to the side. Once they were lying side by side, Julia inched her hand down his chest, through the spattering of hair beneath his navel and reached inside his shorts. She smiled. Things were getting better and better. He followed her lead by trailing a hand slowly down her stomach and sliding a hand toward her panties.

He stroked her and it was as though he'd lit a match. Heat rose and warmed every inch of her body. Flames licked deliciously around his fingers as she increased the pressure of her own hand. He groaned and that inflamed her further.

He shifted his weight and she removed her hand. She opened heavy eyelids to see him pull a fleece comforter and one solitary foil packet from his bag. Not caring that he had thought what was happening now was inevitable, she grinned.

"I didn't..." he began.

Shaking her head, she lifted a finger, beckoning him back beside her. She slipped out of her panties and pulled him down to her. He arranged the comforter over them and encased them in their own private cocoon. He took off his shorts and ripped open the packet.

Smiling, Julia curled her fingers around his and took the protection. Seduction had disappeared, raw need was rife—Julia rolled it onto him before letting her hands linger and stroke once more.

"Now, Daniel. I want you now."

She lay back and he hovered above her. His eyes searching hers, his body strong and rigid. And then, he was inside her, filling her, moving back and forth with a controlled and patient rhythm. Any remaining iota of Julia's reserve vanished as she gripped his buttocks in her hands, pushing him deeper and deeper...

Until he took her to the place she wanted to be.

****

Daniel tapped the scribblings Julia had found at the store up and down against his desk. Leaning back in his chair, he closed his eyes. There had to be something more to link Derek to either the betting shop, the boat or to one of the debt agencies in Kendlewood.

Later, much later, after his and Julia's lovemaking, the conversation had returned to the case. Julia was still adamant she'd seen the type of paper that had been written on somewhere before— but could not figure out where. But this time he was more patient with her, and didn't leave her in the dust while he flew off to find answers.

Daniel pushed away from the desk, and got to his feet. He wasn't going to bring Derek's killer to justice sitting in his office all day. He opened the ever-growing case file and removed the client list he'd requested from Bainbridge. There was no record of Derek having visited the Dial-A-Debt office, but Daniel's gut was still telling him that he had. He snatched up his keys, pocketed the paper Julia had found and headed out the door.

It was nearing the end of the day when Daniel pushed open the agency door and went inside. Bainbridge's secretary smiled up at him.

"Good afternoon, sir. May I help you?"

Daniel glanced at Bainbridge's empty desk. "Gillian, right?"

"Yes, yes it is. Can I help you?"

Daniel smiled. "I'm Detective Inspector Conway, I came in last week and spoke to Mr. Bainbridge. Is he here?"

"He's with a client in the interview room. Can I make an appointment for you, Inspector?"

"No, that's fine. I'm happy to wait."

Daniel lowered himself into one of the overstuffed armchairs and picked up a magazine from the low-level table.

"Would you like a coffee, Inspector?"

He smiled. "That would be great."

Twenty minutes later, Bainbridge emerged from behind a closed door at the back of the office. The way he smiled down at the harassed young woman who walked out with him, turned Daniel's stomach to stone. Debt agencies. They were loan sharks, no matter how they tried to jazz it up. Bainbridge was pond scum. The woman he urged toward the door was so thin and wringing her hands so badly Daniel was convinced a serious nervous breakdown wasn't too far away.

Bainbridge basically made his living tipping desperate people over the edge and leaving them to fall. It gave Daniel huge satisfaction to watch Bainbridge's smile dissolve when he saw Daniel sitting there calmly drinking coffee.

"Inspector Conway. A pleasure to see you again."

He walked forward, his hand extended. Daniel put down his cup, stood, and shook it. Cold. Clammy. Just as he'd expected it to be.

"Could you spare a few minutes, Mr. Bainbridge?"

"Of course. Shall we go into the interview room?"

Daniel walked across the thick carpet and entered Bainbridge's office ahead of him. He waited for the click of the door, then spun around. He bore down on Bainbridge before the man had time to come up with a barrage of transparent excuses.

"What would you say if I told you we have found evidence that Derek Palmer did do business here?"

Bainbridge pulled back his shoulders. "I'd say you were lying."

"Interesting. And what would you say if we'd also found out that Mr. Palmer was not murdered but in fact, attempted suicide as a result of his debts?"

Color rose in the other man's cheeks. "If that has happened, Inspector, it would not be my fault."

"Even though you're in the business of

stretching people's loans to such an astronomical amount that they'd never pay them off even if they lived to ninety-eight years old?"

Bainbridge brushed past Daniel and walked to the opposite side of the room. He crossed his arms. "We offer a service, Inspector. We do not go canvassing for business on the street, people walk in here of their own free will."

Daniel smiled. "So you don't advertise? You don't increase your client's credit limit regardless of whether they ask for it?"

Bainbridge lowered himself into one of the chairs circling the conference table. "What are you trying to say? I'm to be blamed for the whole country's debt problem now?"

Daniel studied him. The eager enthusiasm to help from a few days before had vanished. Bainbridge's tone was arrogant, cocky, and just the incentive Daniel needed to deliver his final blow. He stepped forward and slapped two hands on the table. Bainbridge flinched.

"You've got two minutes to tell me what dealings you had with Derek Palmer before I place you under arrest for obstructing the course of justice. If you choose not to, I will close this business down today and contact every client you have and find out what diabolical rates you offer. Once I've done that, I will see that you come under such a deluge of crippling publicity you'll never recover."

"You can't do that. I've got rights!"

Daniel smiled. "Give me the information I want and you won't need to find out either way, will you?"

Bainbridge's face was livid with color. Daniel continued to glare, his jaw tightly clenched, lips curled back from his teeth. Bainbridge's eyes widened as dots of perspiration shone at his temples. Finally, he threw his hands up.

"Fine. But I am not to blame for that man's

suicide. I want that made perfectly clear."

Daniel pulled out a seat and sat. "Just get on with it," he said, crossing his arms. "I couldn't care less what you want right now."

Bainbridge exhaled a heavy breath. "Derek Palmer came in looking for a loan of £30,000..."

"£30,000?"

"£30,000. He was very honest about the reason for his debt. He told me he had an out-of-control gambling problem and needed the money to pay back someone he owed before they got heavy-handed."

Daniel held up a hand. "So he wanted money from you to pay someone else?"

"Yes. He was scared out of his mind. But I had to say no. Whatever you may think of me, Inspector, I do not encourage people with serious addiction problems to borrow money in order to buy time. I told him to get help, let his family know what sort of trouble he was in."

Daniel's mind raced. If what Bainbridge was saying was true and he had refused the loan, he wasn't the loan shark Suzie thought was involved. Derek had approached him to borrow the money to pay back a loan he had acquired elsewhere. He turned back to Bainbridge.

"So you sent him away without as much as a backward glance. Not your problem, is that it?"

"Inspector—"

Daniel stood and walked to the door. "Save it. Despite the fact that I did not know whether or not you had Derek Palmer as a client when I walked in here..."

"Hey, you said you had evidence that Mr. Palmer was my client," protested Bainbridge.

"No, I asked what would you say if I did. Completely different. Luckily for you, I think you're telling the truth, which means you have eliminated yourself from my inquiries—for the time being."

For the first time since Daniel had arrived, Bainbridge's stiff shoulders relaxed. "I have? Good, that's good. Mr. Palmer was scared, Inspector. Scared for his life and I truly did what I could to help except for the one thing he wanted. Giving him the money."

"Why didn't you tell me this in the first place and save me a lot of time? I could still arrest you for keeping this information from me, you know."

"I didn't tell you because I'd heard about Mr. Palmer's killing on the news." He turned away. "I'm a father, Inspector, and I will not risk my life for anybody other than my children. I knew he was running scared from someone and whoever that someone was could have just as easily come after me."

Daniel nodded. Bainbridge wasn't the first person to feel that way and certainly wouldn't be the last.

"Don't go disappearing anywhere. I may be back."

And with that, Daniel walked from the office and back out into the street. Bainbridge was pretty much out of the loop but Derek had still owed money to someone. Daniel pursed his lips as he slid behind the wheel of his car. He'd just put the key in the ignition when his cell rang. The news on the other end sent adrenaline shooting through his blood.

"Are you *sure*? It's *his* boat? One hundred percent his? No, no, leave it with me. I was about to head over that way. Good work. See you tomorrow."

Daniel snapped the phone shut and took a deep breath. Another piece of the puzzle had inched closer into place. He now knew who owned the boat on which Derek had been killed.

Later that night, Daniel walked through the parking lot of The Ship's Mate. It was Friday and the club was pumping. Music bounced off the walls and the bar staff rushed back and forth as fast as they could, serving drinks and bowls of nachos. Daniel scanned the room but couldn't see Julia anywhere. He guessed she was taking her half way break in her dressing room. He wandered to the bar and managed to squeeze into a space.

Jacob approached him. "What can I get you?"

"A beer would be good."

Jacob snapped off the top of the beer and placed it on the bar. "Wasn't expecting to see you in here again," he said.

"Oh? Why not?"

"Julia told me you were investigating Derek's murder, not courting her."

"Did she?"

"Yeah. So why are you here?"

"Because I'm investigating Mr. Palmer's murder."

Jacob narrowed his eyes. "What are you saying? Someone in here is under suspicion?"

"Maybe."

"You sure like to keep your cards close to your chest, don't you, Inspector?"

Daniel took a gulp of his beer, carefully watching Jacob. "How did you and Derek spend your time together?" he asked.

"Why?"

Daniel shrugged. "Just interested."

"We'd share a bottle of scotch, fish, play cards. You know, guy stuff."

"You fish?"

"Uh-huh."

"You own a boat then?"

Jacob crossed his arms. "I own several boats."

Daniel looked suitably impressed. "Several boats? I didn't realize the club business paid so well."

"It doesn't, but hiring out yachts to rich folks who come out to our little place by the sea every summer does."

Disappointment flooded over Daniel. "You hire them out?"

"Sure. Are you all right?"

Daniel took a deep breath. He'd been sure this latest lead would push the investigation at least a step closer to its conclusion. But once again, it had gotten him nowhere. Unless... He placed a hand on Jacob's arm. "I need your help. Is there somewhere more private we can go talk?"

"Why? What's the matter?" asked Jacob, confusion further creasing his already wrinkled brow.

"Let's just go somewhere quiet, OK?"

Daniel took a seat at Jacob's desk and watched as the older man sat down opposite him. Jacob leaned forward on his elbows.

"So what's all this about?"

Daniel took a deep breath. "We finally managed to track down the yacht on which Derek was shot. We only had Julia's brief description of it so we didn't have a lot to go on, but after a painstaking search we've found it. Forensics uncovered blood spatters on the decking that the killer tried, and failed, to clean. It's Derek's blood, Jacob."

"What are you trying to tell me?"

"The boat is one of yours."

"What? Mine?"

"Yep."

"I don't believe it."

Daniel carefully watched the man in front of him. For Julia's sake, he wanted to believe Jacob had had nothing to do with Derek's death. "So, the first thing I need to know is who hired that boat on the day Derek was killed."

Jacob's face paled to the color of ash. "I leave all

the hiring to Lydia." He stared at Daniel in disbelief. "Derek was killed on *my* boat?"

"Who's Lydia?"

Jacob blew out a long breath. "She's the golden lady who looks after everything to do with my boats."

"It's likely whoever hired the book gave an alias but a description will help. Does Lydia take the bookings?"

But Jacob had already picked up the phone and dialed a number. "Lydia, honey? I need you to check something out for me."

Chapter Eleven

Julia sat in her back garden looking out at the ocean. She'd wracked her brain and still not come up with the origin for the stationery she had found in Derek's store. Daniel and his team were working hard. They'd managed to track the boat back to Jacob. The only job Julia had to do was identify the paper and she couldn't. She blew out a heavy breath.

Last night she had been taking her final bow when she'd spotted Daniel coming down the stairs with Jacob. It was the first time she'd seen him since their night at the Cove. Julia had called the cruise company earlier in the day in an attempt to resign from her new position but it had been hopeless. At first they had thought she was joking. They'd told her in no uncertain terms she had no option but to fulfill her four-month contract.

So that was it. With the decision made for her, Julia had spent the day with her mother. They'd shopped, had lunch, but still Julia could not bring herself to confess her feelings for Daniel to her mom. And with her imminent transfer to the cruise yacht, maybe she'd never have to.

By the time she came back from her post on the ship, there was every possibility Daniel would be in a relationship with someone else. Julia was neither stupid nor blind and had seen for herself just how much female interest there was in Corkley Park's handsome new DI.

The sound of a familiar voice calling her name interrupted her thoughts. She smiled and turned to greet Suzie.

"Hello, stranger." But when she looked at Suzie more closely, her smile slipped. "Hey, are you okay?"

Suzie shook her head. "No. No, I'm not. I've been an idiot. I'm so, so sorry," Suzie sniffed, tears spilling onto her cheeks.

"For what?" Julia stood. "Come here. What's wrong? Aren't you the one who always says nothing is worth crying about?" Julia pulled her friend into her arms and held her close. She held her until Suzie gently stepped back.

"Can we sit down, Julia?" she asked.

"Sure. Shall I get you some water?"

Suzie shook her head. "Oh, Julia, this is so difficult. Why didn't I listen to you?"

Julia sat down beside her on the swing. "I'm guessing this has got something to do with Marcus? Has he hurt you?" she asked, taking her Suzie's hand. "Because if he has—"

Suzie met Julia's eyes. "No, no, it nothing like that. You were right, Julia. He's obsessed with you. He doesn't want me, it was never about me. All he talks about is you. Well, you and Inspector Conway. He's convinced something's going on between you. Is there?"

Heat flooded Julia's cheeks. "No."

"There is! I can tell by your face. Oh, God, but that makes what I've got to tell you even worse." Suzie inhaled a shaky breath and then exhaled her next words in a rush. "I think Marcus knows something about Derek's murder."

"What?" Julia's eyes widened. "Why?"

Suzie reached into her bag and took out a scrap of paper. "I found this by his fireplace."

Julia took the paper and a heavy weight dropped into her stomach. It was the same paper she'd found at Derek's store. Her eyes scanned the few words on the tiny scrap. It was Marcus' writing and for some reason he'd written Derek's name, July

30th and £30,000.

Her hands began to tremble. The paper was from Marcus' bank—that was why she'd recognized it. She had to speak to Daniel. She turned to Suzie. "It's going to be okay. I'll ring Daniel. He'll know what to do."

They hurried into the house and Julia picked up the phone and punched in Daniel's cell number.

"Daniel, it's me. Listen..."

"Hey, you. Sorry I missed you at the club last night."

"It doesn't matter. Listen, I've got something to tell you—"

"I've missed you."

She stole a glance at Suzie before whispering, "I've missed you too, but..."

"I'll try to come round later..."

"Daniel! The paper. From the store. I know where I've seen it. It's the paper the bank uses."

"Which bank?"

"Marcus' bank."

"Marcus? Lowell?"

"Suzie's here. She found more of the same paper in his house. He's obviously tried to burn it. It must be evidence linking him to Derek. Where are you? Shall I bring it to you?"

Daniel cursed. "Hold on, let me think for a second."

Julia looked at Suzie while she waited for Daniel's instruction. She was looking out the kitchen window but Julia could see by the set of her jaw and the trembling in her shoulders that her initial fear had turned to anger. Julia shivered. She had never seen Suzie look so furious. Maybe Suzie wasn't quite the pussycat Julia had thought she was, after all.

"Julia?" said Daniel.

"Yes, I'm here."

"I want you to go with Suzie to the station. Tell

183

the desk sergeant I have sent her there to make a statement. Does Marcus have any clue about her finding that paper?"

Julia checked with Suzie before turning back to the phone. "No, nothing."

"Once she's finished at the station, I want Suzie to go home and pack a bag. Tell her she's to stay with her parents, some friends. She shouldn't be alone—just as a precaution."

Suzie had turned away from the window and was facing Julia with questions raging in her eyes. Julia held out her hand and Suzie took it. She gave her dear friend's fingers an encouraging squeeze. "Is there anything else I can do?" Julia asked Daniel.

"Yes, you can ring Thelma. Do your best not to spook her but tell her I am sending a female officer over there to sit with her and a male officer will be posted outside. If Lowell is involved, I don't want him anywhere near her."

"My God, do you think he'll hurt her?" Julia asked, her eyes locked with Suzie's.

"I've no idea but I'm sending back-up over there right now."

"I'll ring her now. What are you going to do?"

"I'm going to find the son of a bitch."

Julia pressed a hand to the nausea in her stomach. "Be careful."

"I'll be fine. Listen to me. I want you to stay with Suzie until I ring to say I have Lowell in custody, OK?"

Julia hesitated. "If that's what you want."

Julia replaced the phone. She was scared. Scared for Daniel, scared for Suzie, scared for herself.

"Julia?"

She forced a smile and was relieved to see some of the fury in Suzie's face had diminished and her friend looked as afraid as she was. "It's OK, Suze.

Daniel is going to find Marcus and bring him in for questioning, but first we need to get you to the station to make a statement."

"I've got to make a statement? Oh, no, Julia. I can't."

Julia cupped a hand to Suzie's cheek. "It's going to be fine. They'll just want you to tell them what you know about Marcus, that's all."

"You don't seriously believe that?" asked Suzie, incredulously. "Surely you haven't forgiven them for what they did to Phil. What if they set me up? Say I'm involved in some way?"

"Oh, Suze. Come here," Julia said, pulling her in for a hug. "You're going to have to trust them to do the right thing. We both are."

"What if Marcus finds out I've been talking to the police? He could do anything to me," Suzie mumbled against her shoulder.

Julia gave a sad smile. For all her heavy make-up, flashy clothes and sparkly heels, Suzie was the same as anyone else. She had always relied on the brawn of her customers to keep any trouble from her door, but Julia knew Marcus didn't work his way into your brain with actual violence—just the unspoken threat of it. Now he had both her and Suzie afraid of him and it made Julia feel ashamed that he'd managed to get to them the way he had. But it was gratifying to know that if he had anything to do with Derek's death, Daniel would find out and ensure Marcus went to prison for a very long time.

She blew out a breath. "I've got a horrible feeling Derek's murder is about to get uglier, Suze. Marcus likes nothing more than to make money from other people's weaknesses. He loves the position of power the bank gives him. If he is involved, God knows what will happen next."

And then an idea struck her. Julia took a step

back from her friend and held her at arm's length. "Do you know what? You're right. There's no way I'm going to sit around waiting for the police to do all the work."

"What are you going to do?" cried Suzie.

"First I need to call Thelma before the liaison officer arrives at her house. I want to find out if she knew of any business Derek might have had with Marcus. If he arranged for Derek to be killed, he will pay for it—big time. Daniel wanted me to press charges when he assaulted me and I stupidly refused. But murder? No way. He's not getting away with that."

She dialed Thelma's number while Suzie slid onto a stool and dropped her head into her hands. After six rings and the rapid fraying of Julia's nerves, Thelma finally picked up.

"Thelma, it's Julia."

"Well, hello, honey. I just had that nice boyfriend of yours here. We had a lovely chat and a nice cup of tea."

Julia's stomach rolled over and her fingers tightened around the receiver. "My boyfriend?"

"Well, ex-boyfriend then," chuckled Thelma.

"Marcus? He's there?"

"No, he's gone now."

"When did he leave?"

"Is something wrong, dear?"

"Thelma, when did he leave?"

"Oh, um, about an hour ago, I guess. What's wrong?"

Fisting her hair back from her face, Julia blew out a breath. "I hate to be the one to tell you this, but it looks as though Marcus could be involved in Derek's murder."

Silence.

"Thelma? Did you hear what I said?"

"But he was so kind to me. He told me if I need a

visit from the bank's financial advisor to let him know. He seemed genuinely concerned about me. You must be mistaken."

"Did Derek take out a loan with the bank, Thelma? Did Marcus mention anything?"

"Yes, he did, but I was so embarrassed by what Mr. Lowell told me. I had no idea Derek had approached him for a loan. We have no money, Julia. We don't even own this house, we rent it. We have no security."

"So Marcus turned him down?"

"Yes. Oh, wait, there's somebody at the door."

"Wait! It might be Marcus. *Do not* let him back in."

"It looks like the police," she said. "I can see a police car outside."

"Take the phone to the door and let me know if it's them. DI Conway was sending someone over to sit with you."

Julia heard the scuffle of Thelma's movements against the phone and the click of the front door opening. She listened to the introductions with the phone pressed up against her ear. Thelma came back on the line.

"Julia? It's the police, WPC Wilmott is going to look after me."

Julia released the breath she'd been holding. "Try not to worry, Thelma. Tell the police woman what you told me and get her to contact Daniel."

Julia put down the phone and grabbed her keys. She and Suzie raced to the car and made their way to the station. Neither spoke for the twenty minute journey. Julia's heart thumped as her mind raced with new possibilities. If Daniel didn't find Marcus, she knew what she had to do next. And was certain that what she had planned would be too tempting for Marcus to resist.

****

Daniel got out of his car and marched into the bank.

Two other police officers flanked him either side. From what he'd learned about Marcus Lowell, the man was as slippery as an eel and he didn't want to make any mistakes with his arrest. Daniel would make sure he had witnesses and play everything by the book. Nothing would go wrong, even though the image of Marcus' hands around Julia's throat had yet to fade from his mind and he wanted nothing more than a few minutes alone with the guy.

It was lunch hour and the bank buzzed with people. There was a teller at every kiosk, customers were dotted about at the various paying-in machines, and the queues were at least five people deep. The hairs on the back of Daniel's neck prickled—WPC Wilmott had phoned to tell him Lowell had left Thelma's house approximately one hour ago, so Daniel was relying on Lowell coming straight back to the bank.

With a curt nod, he indicated for his officers to follow him toward the information desk. A smiling clerk greeted him.

"May I help you?"

"I wish to speak with Mr. Marcus Lowell, please."

"Do you have an appointment, sir?"

"No, I don't," Daniel said, pulling his ID from his pocket and holding it up. "But I'd appreciate a moment of his time, anyway."

Color darkened her cheeks. "I'm afraid Mr. Lowell isn't here right now. He's due back at three-thirty."

"Do you know where he is?"

"He has a business meeting with managers from two of our other branches."

"Where?"

"I'm sorry?"

"Where is he meeting them?" Daniel could feel himself

losing his patience. "It's important I speak with him immediately."

She stood and called out to an older woman walking purposefully toward a back office. "Sheila? Could you spare a minute, please?"

The woman came closer but Daniel stepped forward before the information clerk could speak. "Are you the assistant manager?"

She flicked a glance to the clerk before turning back to Daniel and smiling graciously. "Is there a problem, sir?"

Daniel flashed his badge. "Marcus Lowell. Where is he?"

"He left for a meeting in Salisbury this morning. He's due back at three-thirty. If I can be of any help, Inspector..."

"Salisbury? But that's over an hour's drive away."

"Yes, the meeting started at eleven."

Frustration burned inside him. "I know for a fact Mr. Lowell never went to that meeting." He turned to the other officers. "Go to Lowell's house. Make sure he's not there and make no mistakes. If he's there, you arrest him. Take him back to the station and await further instruction. Is that clear?"

The officers nodded and quickly left. Daniel turned back to the assistant manager. "I want access to Mr. Lowell's office. I am going to arrange for a search warrant to be brought over but I would very much appreciate your co-operation in the meantime. This is possibly a case of life or death."

She paled. "Of course, Inspector. Right this way."

Daniel followed her through to a back office, his mind racing. The piece of paper Julia had recognized and the scrap Suzie had found meant Lowell knew something. He might not have been the one to fire the shot that had killed Derek, but Daniel's gut was telling him Lowell was in this up to his neck. Could Lowell feel the net closing in on him? Is that why he had paid a visit to Thelma this morning? To find out what she knew?

The assistant manager led him into Lowell's office. Carefully, he closed the door behind them. She stood with her hands clasped tightly together in front of her.

"What can I do to help, Inspector?"

"I'm looking for anything mentioning a Mr. Derek Palmer, or loan agreements or any kind of abnormal paperwork."

"May I ask what this is all about?"

"Believe me, all will be revealed soon enough."

After an hour of searching through Lowell's domain, Daniel had enough paperwork to know Lowell was, at the minimum, involved in after-hours money lending. The deputy manager confirmed the papers were not bank policy and they made no sense to her whatsoever. Upon further investigation, the two of them managed to conclude Lowell had been using the bank's money to make high-interest loans of his own.

Lowell had had Derek Palmer right where he wanted him—broken and in debt. The rage Daniel had previously felt for the man was nothing compared to what pumped through his veins now. Daniel instinctively knew Lowell had arranged for Derek to be killed. His father had been killed by an assassin. Paid killers hired by cowards too damn scared to do their own dirty work, too afraid to feel the guilt of someone else's blood on their hands. The man who had arranged his father's death might still be out there somewhere, but Derek's killer wouldn't be for much longer.

Daniel left the bank and sprinted to his car.

Once inside, he made a call to the station asking for a status report from every officer out looking for Marcus. As he waited for the information to come through, he looked out the windscreen at the workers, shoppers, mothers and children filing back and forth. Corkley Park was a place made for family, a place to settle in your twilight years or the perfect place for a proposal on the beach.

After everything Daniel had seen and done, never did he think a case like this would be the one to taint his record. He'd always assumed if a felon was ever likely to escape him, it would be when he was an officer in the city. It was every cop's nightmare to have to trace a serial killer or a missing child, but to have the killer of an elderly man elude him in a sleepy coastal town? It made him look completely inept. He slammed his palm against the steering wheel just as the radio crackled.

He listened intently to the progress report but once it finished, Daniel would not have described it as a progress anything. Lowell was still on the run. Daniel closed his eyes and took a moment to think.

Jacob's assistant at the boat hire company had said the man who had hired the boat had been tall with dark hair. Could it have been Marcus? Her description was sketchy at best but it was now a definite possibility.

Daniel pulled out of the parking lot, pressed hard on the accelerator and sped to the marina where they had tracked down Jacob's boat. By the time he arrived, it was nearing six o'clock and several boats were coming in to moor. The sunlight glinted from the windows and chrome of the yachts, while the great sweeping sails of others could be seen far out on the water. Any other time the sight would have been breathtaking. But not to Daniel. Not today.

Lifting a hand to shield his eyes from the sun as

it neared the horizon, Daniel looked around the yard and spotted a woman in her early forties issuing orders.

"Excuse me, are you Lydia?" he asked, holding out his ID.

She glanced at it before turning back to the young lad she had been talking to. She promptly dumped a huge coil of rope into his arms. "Go put that in the warehouse and then get yourself home. You did a good day's work today—I'm proud of you."

She watched him walk away before rubbing the dust from

her hands on denim overalls before extending one to Daniel.

"Lydia Marshall, Inspector. Pleased to meet you. Why don't you come into the office?"

In the tiny portable cabin, Daniel slid into a plastic chair. "I was there when Jacob spoke to you on the phone," he began. "You told him you didn't know either of the men who hired or took out the boat on the day Derek Palmer was killed. Is that right?"

"Yep, I'd never seen the man or the lady before."

She may as well have punched him in the face. "Lady?"

"I didn't recognize either of them."

"What lady?"

"The lady who took the boat out. Never seen her before."

He looked at her in disbelief. "Jacob never mentioned a woman. Did you tell him it was a woman?"

"No, but he didn't ask."

"For crying out loud!" Daniel cried, leaping to his feet. "This changes everything."

Lydia had jumped up too. "I'm sorry but it's no good yelling at me or Jacob, Inspector. Isn't it your job to be asking the right questions?"

Daniel glared at her. She was right. He should've been asking the questions but he had been too bloody busy worrying about spending time with Julia to think deeper about the case. How could he have not questioned Lydia himself?

"Describe her to me. The color of her hair, build, anything."

"Well, that was just it. She was obviously trying to dress like a man for some reason. Dressed all in black she was. Head to toe. I could just see a few blond strands of her hair at the sides but that was it."

"Why didn't you come forward with this information?"

"I meant to—"

"For Christ's sake! Don't tell me I can't yell at you now. Do you know how important this is? I have wasted days assuming Derek Palmer's killer was a man."

"I'm sorry. I have a record, I didn't want the cops—"

Daniel squeezed his eyes shut. "Save it. Did you personally know Derek Palmer? Was he there when the woman came in to get the keys?"

"He was there, yes. I didn't know him, but after Jacob described him to me, I knew it was the man waiting out in the courtyard. He never actually came into the office."

"Did he look anxious, on edge?"

"No, not at all—in fact, he looked like a kid in a candy shop. The lady who took him out the yacht was all smiles, saying it was a birthday treat for her dad."

"And how did she explain the absence of the man who paid to hire the boat? Did she mention him at all?"

"She said he was her brother but had been called away on business. She was disappointed they

193

wouldn't all be sharing the trip."

Daniel shoved a hand through his hair. "You need to think long and hard, Lydia. Try to describe everything you can remember about the man who originally hired the boat. What he looked liked, what he said. And then you need to think some more and tell me everything about the woman."

Ten minutes later, Daniel bounded down the iron steps of the office. The man who'd hired the boat was Lowell. Adrenaline pumped through Daniel's blood like oil through an engine. Surely nothing could stop him nailing the son of a bitch against the wall now. But as he slid behind the wheel of his car, his phone rang and a knot of apprehension settled low in his stomach.

"Ah, Inspector Conway. What a pleasure to talk to you at last."

Lowell. "You've got some nerve, Lowell. Where are you, you bastard?"

"I see you and your pathetic police force have been running all over town looking for me." He laughed. "It's been so much fun watching you all."

Daniel's jaw tightened. "I know it was you who arranged for Derek Palmer to be killed, Lowell. You can bet your ass I'll find you and when I do, you'll pay."

"And how are you treating my Julia? I hope you don't think you'll be laying your dirty hands on her. She's mine. Have I not already made that perfectly clear?"

"You're delusional," said Daniel, looking up at the windows of the surrounding buildings and wondering whether Lowell was watching him right this second. "Julia does not love you and never will. How did it feel when you found out she'd seen Derek killed? That must have messed up your plans big time."

"Not at all. It added to the thrill of it all, if you

must know. Don't you know her brother was killed by a police officer?"

"Yes, she's told me."

"She'll never be with you, you fool. Julia already knows she's mine. In fact, I've started taking steps to make sure she understands that completely."

Chapter Twelve

Julia watched Daniel enter the club. At six feet two, his broad frame gave her the advantage of seeing him above the heads of the other patrons. His face was set in grim determination, his shoulders so tense they were bunched almost to his jaw. With her heart thundering hard against her chest, she concentrated on finishing her song and not alerting anyone to Daniel's obvious agitation.

His eyes locked onto her like a human tracker beam and he came toward her with such purposeful steps, she was anxious he was going to march straight onto the stage—and he did.

"Daniel? What are you...?"

He took the microphone from her hand and pushed it back into its stand, then took her hand and pulled her down the steps and off the platform.

"Daniel!"

He ignored both Julia's and the crowd's protests. Angry indignation quickly replaced her initial fear of more bad news. She snatched her hand from his iron grip and only then did he stop and face her. She fisted her hands at her hips.

"What the hell do you think you're doing? How dare you drag me around the place like a bloody caveman."

"I haven't got time for this, Julia," he said, through clenched teeth.

"Time for what? Time to stop you from breaking my arm?"

His gaze locked with hers and despite her outrage, she instinctively took a step back. Fire burned and fury stormed in his eyes and a faint pulse beat at his temple. His breath escaped in short, sharp pants from his open mouth. She swallowed. Something had happened. Something serious.

"What is it? What's wrong?" she asked.

"Didn't I ask you to stay with Suzie until I had Lowell under arrest?"

Julia's hand shot to her chest. "Oh God, is she all right?"

Daniel lifted a hand to his head. "How the hell would I know? I've got officers trying to track her down right now. But what about you? It's you I'm talking about!"

"But, I'm—"

"No, Julia, no buts," he said. "Jesus."

Her own anger clawed at her throat. He was acting like Marcus, acting like he owned her. "Now hang on a minute..."

Jacob's appearance at her side cut her off mid-sentence.

"Does someone want to tell me what's going on?" Can you hear that lot?" he asked, jabbing a thumb in the direction of the audience behind him. "I'm going to have a riot on my hands if you don't get back up on that stage and finish what you started."

After a long moment, Daniel broke his gaze with Julia and turned to Jacob.

"Julia will be going back out there tonight. She's coming with me."

Julia laughed wryly and crossed her arms. "Am I really?"

He reached out and wrapped his fingers firmly around her elbow. "Yes. You are."

She yanked her arm from his grip. "Not until you tell me what's going on, I'm not."

He turned away from her and looked at Jacob. "There have been certain developments in Derek's

197

case and Julia needs to come with me right now. I have to get her out of here."

Julia stepped in front of him because apparently Daniel could no longer see her. "I'm not going anywhere, Daniel."

"Damn it, Julia—"

"I can only assume by this act of macho bullying, police tactic that I'm in danger. Am I right?"

The two of them glared at each other.

Jacob cleared his throat. "Why don't you take the Inspector up to the office, Julia? Get changed and then get out of here? It seems to me Inspector Conway isn't the type to come in throwing his weight around unless it was necessary."

She spun around to face Jacob. "He's a cop, isn't he? What else do you expect?"

With that, she turned on her heel and headed for the stairs. She walked into her dressing room, knowing Daniel was right behind her. She flinched when the door slammed shut and he began pacing the room in front of her like a caged animal. Julia's own body was wired with tension as she watched him.

"Well? What's going on?" she demanded.

Abruptly he stopped. Her heart beat loudly in her ears, and for the first time since he'd stormed into the club, she looked properly into his eyes. It wasn't anger burning behind them. It was fear, fear for her. Her anger melted into comprehension. She saw now that he was there because he cared enough to insist she listen to him.

"It's Lowell," he said. "He's still on the run. He's going to come after you, Julia. I know it.

Julia swallowed her own dread, and took a slow step forward. "He can try but there's no way he's going to get close enough to hurt me."

Daniel looked at her. "And how do you figure that when we have no idea where he is? He could—"

198

She smiled gently, lifted a hand to his locked jaw. "Because I'll be with you, won't I?"

He exhaled a breath, a faint smile briefly touching his lips. "Yeah, I suppose you will."

She reached up and pressed a kiss to his mouth. "I'm sorry. I should've stayed with Suzie."

He smoothed a hand down a length of her hair. "Yes, you should have."

"She told me she was going straight to her mom's. Let me get changed and we'll get out here, OK?"

She turned and walked into the bathroom, stripping off her pirate clothes as she went. She changed into jeans and a T-shirt and as she was pulling her hair back with a bandanna, ventured back out into the room.

He stood with his back to her. His head tipped forward, his strong hands splayed above the pockets of his jeans. She went to him. Dropping her head to his back, she clasped her hands around his waist and offered her strength. Slowly she felt the tension seep from his shoulders. He turned around so she was standing within the circle of his arms and lowered his hand to the curve of her waist. After a few moments, he broke the silence—his voice quietly controlled.

"Lowell arranged for Derek to be murdered."

Her breath caught in her throat but she bit back the urge to scream out, to rant and rave, to punch and kick.

"I don't have proof yet but I'm sure Derek was lured to the boat either by the temptation of an exclusive poker game or maybe a promise of wiping out his debts forever. We'll probably never know exactly what got him there." He paused and Julia felt him shudder. "Lowell has been using the bank's funds to organize high interest loans for people who are in dire need of money. People who have no security, no way of borrowing money from an organization that will do their best to help them. In short, Lowell is the lowest of the low."

He dropped his hands and turned to face her. His fingers softly cradled her chin and she reached up to cover his hands with her own.

"I don't know what to say," she said. "Marcus arranged for him to be killed? But the man with the gun...?"

"It wasn't a man. It was a woman dressed to look like a man."

"A woman? Oh, my God, so all this time you've been looking for a man and it was a woman? You must want to thump me."

"Of course I don't. You've always said you never had a clear look at the shooter. It was done as a decoy, Julia. None of this is your fault."

But his words didn't matter, she felt entirely to blame.

"It must've been someone that Derek knew, or at least an arranged trip, because the woman who gave the killer the keys to the boat that day said Derek was happy, relaxed. There was no sign at all that he felt under threat."

Julia closed her eyes and drew the picture of that day to her mind's eye. The person with the gun was a woman. It made more sense now. The vanity, the struggle getting Derek's body over the side of the boat. But still she couldn't identify who it was. All she could see was the black clothes.

She pressed her fingers to her closed lids. "I feel so useless."

He rubbed her shoulder. "Don't. We'll find him. But the most important thing right now is to get you out of here."

She looked into his eyes and nausea swept through her chest and into her mouth. "Marcus hasn't finished with me, has he?"

Daniel moved his hands and gripped her wrists. "No, but you're going to stay with me until we find him. You can move into my house and then I'll know you're safe."

"You're a detective, Daniel, not a police protection officer. I can't let you waste your expertise babysitting me."

"Listen to me. He's told me he wants you, and if he has his way he will have you by whatever means necessary."

"But how can I move in with you? What will your superiors say if they find out?"

"It's just one night, Julia. You're leaving tomorrow, and to be perfectly honest, this trip is becoming a blessing in disguise. God knows I don't want you to go but if it means putting miles of ocean between you and Lowell, so be it."

They left the club and jumped into Daniel's car. He gunned the engine and headed back to Julia's house. As they got out of the car and ran up the pathway, he put a hand to the base of her back.

"Grab a few essentials and we'll head back to my place. I can coordinate the team from there. The officers who have been working all day have gone home for some much needed sleep—the new team already know the main objective is to find Lowell. If it's you he wants, he won't have gone far."

She nodded and their gazes locked. He brushed a finger along her jaw before bending and pressing a soft kiss to her lips. "It's going to be all right, I promise."

Julia turned and put the key to the lock, but the door swung open on its own. She turned wide eyes to Daniel. He put a finger to his lips and drew his gun from the concealed halter at his side before pushing his way in front of her.

He pulled Julia behind him and they entered the house. Daniel walked ahead, slowly pushing open the door to the living room and kitchen, but each room was empty, nothing touched or disturbed. Julia kept her hand glued to his back, her entire body humming with adrenaline. Marcus had been there. His evil had leaked into the paint on the walls, permeated the fabric of the drapes and sunk into the pile of the carpets. She could feel him everywhere.

Daniel turned and indicated they were going upstairs. Step by excruciating step, Julia followed him to the upper level of the house. But after checking the bathroom and the spare room, it became clear Marcus had already left. They walked into Julia's bedroom and when she flicked on the light, Julia gasped, no doubt in her mind that Marcus had completely lost his mind.

She fought from Daniel's grip and ripped her parents' photographs from the wall. Marcus had taken their pictures from the frames sitting at her bedside and pinned them crudely to the wall. He'd then taken a gun and shot each of them through the head.

Tears burned her eyes and her hands violently shook.

"Daniel, he's going to kill them. We have to do something. He's going to kill them!"

But Daniel had already pulled his phone from his pocket. "Their address, Julia? I need their address."

She quickly told him.

"This is DI Conway, I want officers sent over to twenty-five Harden's Mead immediately. Marcus Lowell has been to Julia Kershaw's home and left a clear message he intends to harm her parents. I am taking Miss Kershaw into protective custody right away. I want an immediate report of her parents' status as well as having them removed from the house. Do I make myself clear?" He flicked a glance at Julia before turning his back to her. "I also want an officer put outside my house. There's every possibility Lowell will come to my place looking for Miss Kershaw. What? No, she's staying with me. Don't ask questions, just do it!"

He snapped the phone shut and turned to Julia, sitting on the bed, rocking back and forth. He dropped to his knees in front of her and took her hands. Gently, he pressed his lips to her knuckles.

"We need to get out of here, Julia."

She lifted her head. "What if we're too late, what if he's killed them?"

"Julia, listen to me." He stroked the hair from her eyes. "Lowell has no gain from harming your parents. This is more for my benefit than yours. He's obsessed and angry. He knows the net is closing in on him and doesn't know how to stop it. Now come on. Let's go."

She pushed his hand away and leapt to her feet. "I want to go to my parents' house. I have to see them, make sure they're safe."

She was about to push passed him when his cell went off. They both stopped.

"DI Conway." He flicked a glance at Julia. "They're OK?" A small smile and a nod.

Relief flooded over her, crippling her legs and pushing her to the floor. They were alive—for now. But there was no way Julia was risking Marcus killing them. The plan that had been manifesting in her brain had just been pushed forward a gear. She would go back to Daniel's but once he was asleep, she would do things her way.

What did it matter? So what if she pissed him off so much he never spoke to her again? It would be a blessing. It would be an end to her clinging to the desperate hope that they had a future together. A relationship with Daniel would hurt too many people, including herself. It was a job that involved guns, risks and heartache. Julia had seen her

203

mother suffer over the loss of a child. How could she subject herself to losing the man she loved to a bullet one day?

****

Julia cradled the phone between her ear and shoulder as she tried to calm her mother's hysteria. She watched Daniel throw pasta into a saucepan and wondered how he expected her to eat when she had a huge lump of fear lodged in her throat.

"Mom, everything is going to be OK. The police will find Marcus and arrest him. No, this is not your fault. Mom, you've got to calm down and listen to me." Julia walked from the kitchen into the hallway. She lowered her voice. "I'm not going to let anything happen to either you or Dad, do you understand? I should have listened to that voice in my head telling me to get away from Marcus weeks ago."

"But it was me who kept on saying what a good match he was for you," cried her mother. "How could I have been so blind?"

"It's OK, Mom. We'll sort Marcus Lowell out once and for all. You'll see."

"We? Who's we?" asked her mother.

"Daniel...I mean the police. Inspector Conway's team is looking for him around the clock. They'll find him and arrest him."

"Funny how they don't just shoot scum like Marcus Lowell dead, like they did my son."

Julia squeezed her eyes shut. "Mom, please."

Her mother released a long breath. "And I suppose you're still intent on leaving me within the next day or so?"

"The cruise liner leaves tomorrow, Mom and I *will* be on it." She paused. "There's nothing I want to stay here for, Mom. Leaving Corkley Park is the best thing in the world for me right now."

She heard a shuffle of feet behind her. She turned to see Daniel watching her, a spoon of steaming tomato and basil sauce in his hand. He didn't flinch when a drop splashed onto his bare foot. Julia swallowed, keeping her eyes level with his.

"Are you sure?" her mother was saying. "Because I've heard the rumors, you know?"

"What rumors, Mom?" Julia asked, quietly.

"About you and that policeman."

Guilty heat surged in Julia's cheeks and heart.

"Nothing is going on between me and DI Conway, Mom. I would never date a policeman, you know that. Not after Phil."

The intensity in Daniel's eyes mixed with her mother's sad silence over the phone was more than Julia could stand. Dropping her gaze to the floor, she wiped a stray tear from her cheek.

"I have to go," she said, her voice breaking. "DI Conway has already said it would be best if we didn't speak again until Marcus is caught. Do what the police say, OK? I love you."

"Julia?"

"Yes?"

"I was wrong about Marcus and although it pains me to say it, I could be wrong about other things too."

Julia lifted her head and looked at Daniel.

"I'll bear that in mind, Mom. I promise."

Sitting at the kitchen table, Julia and Daniel shared the simple meal of pasta and sauce Daniel had prepared. She managed to eat half a dozen mouthfuls before placing her knife and fork together on her plate. The food felt like lead in her stomach. She picked up her wineglass and took a sip while watching Daniel.

Her nerves were stretched to breaking point and the reason wasn't only due to Marcus' disappearance. Daniel's eyes when she'd been speaking to her mother had told Julia everything she needed to know. Her undeniable and very real feelings for him were entirely reciprocated.

But she'd had to do it—had to say the things she'd said. How else was she supposed to walk away from him tomorrow unless she left him little choice but to turn and walk in the opposite direction? Hadn't he said it would be best for her to be on the Princess II and away from here?

To pursue their relationship felt useless, not to mention selfish. She had to bear in mind her parents' feelings, and what about the circumstances in which she and Daniel had met? Feelings had been running high every moment since Derek was shot and killed. Who was to say their love for each other would be as hot once the problems around them had cooled?

She'd convinced herself that a career beyond Corkley Park was what she needed, but as she looked at Daniel's furrowed brow, she knew she'd be more than happy continuing to sing at the club, laughing with friends and spending her time with him. In fact, nothing seemed more appealing.

"Are you all right?"

She blinked and gave a faint, yet forced smile. "Sure."

"You were miles away."

"I was considering everything we already know," she said, thinking it a better option to tell him what she'd been thinking earlier in the day, than now. "The fact that Marcus used Jacob's boat business, that I witnessed the killing. Do you think Marcus might have planned for me to see it?"

"He couldn't have known you'd be there."

"God, I hope not. The thought he may have been planning Derek's killing when I was with him makes me sick."

She took another sip of her wine.

Daniel put down his own knife and fork. "Why don't you go upstairs and have a bath. It might make you feel better."

She met his eyes and smiled. "That sounds so tempting. Are you sure you wouldn't mind?"

He pushed his chair back, stood and held out a hand. "Come on. I'll show you where everything is."

They mounted the stairs and Daniel led her into his bedroom. It was masculine, yet not too much so. Julia was struck by the scent of him everywhere. It hung in the air around them—the perfect blend of sandalwood, fresh air and pine. She inhaled deeply as he wandered into the en-suite and the sound of running water filled the room.

He handed her a big, fluffy towel. "Here. I'm sure you'll want to use your own things but feel free to help yourself to anything else." His eyes lingered on her lips. He blew out a breath. "Right then, I'll leave you to it."

Don't leave, she wanted to scream, *stay with me.* "OK."

He walked to the door. Stopped. Turned. "How about another glass of wine?"

She smiled at his raised eyebrow and smiled. "That would be nice."

He gave her a wink and left, pulling the door gently closed behind him.

Ten minutes later, Julia slipped beneath the water and let the water rise to her collar bone. Despite her futile attempt to distance herself from him, her body still craved Daniel like a tonic. She wanted to make love to him one last time. Her need wasn't just physical, but emotional, spiritual, filling every part of her with a desperate necessity. She suddenly needed to be joined with him more than she needed oxygen.

She heard a knock at the door. "Your wine, Mademoiselle."

She smiled at his courtesy. A lesser man would have barged in, hoping to catch a glimpse of a woman naked in the bath. "Come in."

He paused before he pushed the door open. Desire surged through her as he stepped into the room. The lack of feminine bubbles meant every inch of her body was visible to him and his attention lingered everywhere possessively. Neither of them spoke for a long moment before he blinked and finally met her eyes.

He walked forward and placed the glass on a small side table. "Enjoy. I'll be downstairs."

He moved to walk away but Julia shot out a hand and gripped his muscular forearm. "Stay with me, Daniel."

"Julia, this isn't a good idea..."

"Please. Don't go."

He raised his eyes to the ceiling, muttering something incoherent before turning his gaze back to hers. "I love you, Julia. You can't ask me to make love to you, touch you after telling your mother there's nothing left for you here."

"I'm sorry. I had to say something."

"Not that. You didn't have to say that."

The pain in his eyes pierced her heart, making her feel cold and ashamed. She could feel him tremble and softened her grip. "I didn't think—"

He closed his eyes for a second before opening them again. "There's nothing more I want to do than lift you from that bath and take you right here, right now. Don't think I don't want to hold your soaking wet, beautiful body to mine and make love to you over and over again."

"Then do it, Daniel. Please."

He held up a hand and her breath caught in her throat to see his eyes shining with tears. He swallowed.

"I can't. Not when you still want to leave so badly." He shook his head. "Not when you can walk away from me like I mean absolutely nothing to you."

"But you said my leaving was a good idea too."

"No, I said it made sense for you to leave, not that I want you to go. There is a world of difference between logic and love."

He turned and left the room. Julia stared at the back of the closed door for a long time before sinking beneath the surface and letting her own hot tears merge with the water.

Chapter Thirteen

Julia lay on her back, listening to the steady rhythm of Daniel's breathing beside her. It was approaching two o'clock in the morning and she had feigned sleep for the last two hours while waiting for Daniel's restlessness to settle into something close to slumber. Her heart thumped hard inside her chest and her fingers clutched the quilt. Their evening had consisted of stilted conversation and unspoken declarations. Finally, she'd gone up to bed at midnight. Daniel had climbed beneath the covers just half an hour later.

When he'd brushed her hair softly from her face and kissed her temple, a solitary tear had dissolved into her pillow knowing she was about to betray his wishes so badly. She had no idea if her plan was going to work but she had to try. She had to do something to ensure Marcus did not get away with Derek's murder.

She inched out of bed and tip-toed to the bathroom. Quickly she changed from pajamas back into her jeans. Her reflection pretty much summed up the way she felt. Dark circles stood out against her pale skin, her hair lay disheveled and unkempt around her head. Inhaling a shaky breath, she hitched the bag onto her shoulder and left the room.

Knowing she had to dodge the policeman keeping watch outside the house, she crept downstairs and dropped to her knees in the den. She then crawled on all fours to the window and peered outside. He wasn't around the back at that moment but knew he was continually circling the property.

She slid the window open a crack and waited for the sound of his footsteps. It wasn't long before they became louder and then softened as he rounded the side of the house for another circuit.

She scrambled to her feet, then pushed the window open a few more vital inches before sliding over the sill on her belly and gently lowering herself to the soft grass beneath. In her bare feet, Julia sprinted across the lawn and over the hedge that surrounded Daniel's small garden. She had a long run to her house and prayed she managed to get there without being followed by the duty officer.

As she ran along the deserted road, her senses were on high alert to every sound and movement. Once she was a safe distance from Daniel's house, she slipped on her shoes. Pressing a hand to the cramp in her side, she pulled out her cell. She tapped her foot up and down as the phone rang repeatedly in her ear.

"Come on, come on. Answer it, damn it."

But the answer phone kicked in. "This is Marcus Lowell, I am unavailable right now but please feel free to leave a message."

Even the sound of his voice made her stomach lurch. She coughed. "Marcus? It's me. Look, I've been back to my house and seen the pictures of my Mom and Dad. Why are you doing this? Please meet me and tell me what I have to do to make you stop. I'm begging you, please—"

She heard a click and he was on the line. "Ah-ha. The wanderer returns. How are you, Julia?"

Gripping the phone, she exhaled a breath. "Marcus, thank God."

"What's the matter, sweetheart? You sound kind of shaken. Is Detective Inspector Conway not looking after you properly?"

"Why did you do that to my parents' pictures, Marcus?"

"What did I do?"

Anger simmered beneath the surface of Julia's skin. So he wanted to play, just as he always did. "I know you're angry I called our relationship off but I will not accept you threatening my parents, Marcus. They have the police looking after them right now. Have you any idea how that must feel to my mother?"

"I wasn't the one who caused this to happen, Julia. You were."

But as he talked, she pressed the phone closer to her ear. She could hear a female voice in the background, she was sure of it. "Who's that?" she asked. "Have you got someone with you?"

He laughed. "Oooh, are you jealous?"

"Of course not."

"No? Well, if you will insist on ringing me in the middle of the night you never know who I'm going to be with..." He let the sentence hang.

"I thought you were dating Suzie now," Julia said, in her friend's defense. "Or is that her?"

"No, it's not Suzie, Julia. I'm not into exclusivity unless I'm with you. No one means to me what you do."

"Suzie really likes you, Marcus. A lot. You should let her go. Let her find someone who loves her back," Julia said, angrily. "It's not fair. She doesn't deserve to be treated this way."

He sighed. "Please don't tell me what to do, Julia. It will only annoy me."

Calm, Julia, stay calm. She changed the subject. "Will you meet me? Maybe we can work our differences out? Try again?"

"Try again?" he laughed. "Even after I shot a bullet through your parents' heads? So to speak."

"Marcus, please."

A long pause. Julia heard his breathing quicken. "Where are you, Julia?" he asked, quietly.

"I was with Daniel but I've managed to get away."

He let out a low whistle. "Well, well, maybe I was wrong about the two of you. Is his goody-goody charm becoming a little repulsive?"

"I never had feelings for him in the first place, Marcus. I told you that. Look, will you meet me or not?"

"I can't. It's too risky."

She swallowed. "What is?"

"The police think I had something to do with Derek Palmer's murder. Ridiculous, isn't it?"

"Did you?"

There was a momentary silence. "You shouldn't ask me things like that, Julia. You haven't a clue about anything."

Her thoughts snapped back to the woman with him. "You know, the police are now saying it was woman who shot Derek."

"A woman?" He laughed. "Is that what Inspector Conway thinks? Even after you told him it was a man? He isn't giving you a lot of credit as a witness, is he, darling?"

But instead of answering she strained to hear the now muffled female voice in the background. All she could make out was the distinct sound of a door slamming.

"So, what happens now?" asked Marcus, in a far too breezy voice. He was scared. Julia was sure of it.

She had to deal with this in Marcus' mind set, not her own. Blowing out a breath, she tried again. "This is crazy, Marcus. I want to talk to you face to face. You can't carry on like this. Someone's going to get hurt and I know you don't want that."

"It doesn't matter what I want anymore. If the police catch me, they're going to throw away the key. You know they don't care whether they've got the right person or not, don't you, sweetheart?"

"But—"

"They'll pin it on me if that's what they want. They would've planted evidence or something, no doubt."

"Maybe I can help," Julia said, quickly. "I will testify in court it wasn't you who pulled the trigger."

"Ah, you'd do that for little old me? I'm touched."

"The point is, Marcus, it will do you no good to run away."

"I am not running away, I am merely keeping a low profile."

Julia's mind was working overtime trying to come up with a way to get him to meet her, trust her. All she needed to do was arrange a meeting and Daniel could be there to arrest him. "Why don't I check into a bed and breakfast out of town? I'll ring you with the address and you come over tomorrow?"

"What about the police?"

"They'll have no clue. I'm going to turn off my cell so they'll have no way of tracking me."

He hesitated. "Fine, I'll catch up with you sometime tomorrow."

She blew out a breath. "Good. We'll talk then. We'll get this all straightened out, Marcus. I promise."

"Julia?"

"Yes?"

"I'm sorry for doing that to your parents' pictures. I don't know what has happened to me since I fell so hard for you. Everything is going wrong and I'm beginning to feel as though I've got nothing left."

She lifted her eyes to the ink-black sky, sending up a silent prayer asking God to make this work. He was so unstable, so unpredictable. "I know, I know. But you can still have me, Marcus. As a friend, if nothing else."

"A friend, Julia?" He laughed. "I think I need

considerably more than that."

She swallowed, feeling the mood shift once more. "We're in this together now, Marcus. I won't let you down."

"No, Julia—I know you won't."

The line went dead and Julia exhaled a heavy breath. There was no turning back, the wheels had been set in motion. Part of her was scared but another deep, more determined part knew she had no alternative but to carry this forward. No one was going to threaten her family or stop her from living the life she wanted to. Marcus had murdered a man, threatened her parents, used Suzie. Julia had had enough.

****

Daniel reached for his phone, trying to silence it before it woke Julia.

"Hello?" he mumbled. "What?!"

He snapped his head around and saw the empty space beside him. He threw back the covers and ran into the bathroom, the phone still at his ear.

"Why the hell didn't you break down the door if I didn't hear you knocking?" he yelled. "Yes, yes, you were right to go straight after her. You've no idea who she was speaking to? No? Right, I'm on my way. *Do not* lose sight of her."

He snapped the phone shut and fought his fury at Julia's disappearance and his own humiliation at falling asleep. How could he have been so stupid? He should've known she would not stay put.

By the time he'd dressed and pulled the door shut behind him, his pulse was beating hard at his temple and a line of icy cold sweat had formed on his spine. Thank God he'd requested someone to watch the house—the woman was not only a danger to herself, it was a wonder he hadn't suffered a heart attack himself.

As Daniel checked and double-checked the

ammo in his gun, he rushed through the front door. The officer who'd been stationed outside was following her down the deserted path that led into town. For once, Daniel wished he'd bought a town house on a main road rather than the discreet vacation-type home he'd had to have the minute he'd laid eyes on it.

He brushed a hand through his hair. He'd seen Julia's terrorized expression when she'd been faced with her parents' gruesome pictures, but he'd also seen her raw determination when he'd left her alone in the bath tub. She'd been hurt and angry at his rejection and he knew with Julia, anger quickly became action. He should have known she would try something like this—she was the type of woman who took matters into her own hands. She'd proven that several times over the few days he'd known her.

Apparently, she'd spoken to someone on her cell. Lowell? Did she know where he was? But then he saw her up ahead and slowed his pace. If anything happened to her, he had no idea how he'd get over it. He loved her. He loved her more than he'd ever loved anyone else. She was the most selfish, crazy, inconsiderate...caring, protective, passionate woman he had ever met and he wanted to make her his forever. He blinked against the sudden stinging in his eyes. God knew how he'd get through the next four months without her, but he would. And when she came back? He would present her with a proposal she couldn't refuse.

The tracking officer would be somewhere to his right. Daniel scanned the silhouette of the trees until he spotted him. Daniel gestured for him to come over.

Once the young officer was at his side, Daniel put an arm around his shoulder. "We'll let her go on ahead. If she was talking to Lowell, there's every chance he'll want to see her. I've got no idea why she left or what she's got planned. But this will not end badly, do you hear me? This will not end badly."

The young officer nodded curtly. "Understood, sir."

Daniel watched Julia as she hurriedly walked on. Her head darted left and right, her steps unsteady and hesitant. Daniel and the officer continued behind her for the next ten minutes or so when a car approached from up ahead. Both Daniel and the officer jumped under the cover of the trees. Julia did the same.

But the driver had obviously already seen her as he pulled up at the exact spot where she'd disappeared. Daniel's jaw tightened as he watched Lowell exit the car. But when he saw who got out of the passenger side, shock reverberated through him until his blood boiled with suppressed anger.

In that moment, Daniel knew it was Suzie who had shot Derek Palmer in cold blood.

He pulled his gun from its holster as Suzie ducked one way into the trees, Lowell the other. Daniel gestured for the young officer to come closer. "I'll focus on Lowell, you keep with the woman. No matter what, do not lose her. She is no doubt armed and dangerous. I am trusting you to keep her well away from Miss Kershaw."

"Yes, sir."

Daniel gave a nod and the officer disappeared silently into the trees. Cocking his own gun, Daniel followed Lowell.

Within seconds, he halted upon hearing Julia's voice.

"Marcus?" she asked, in apparent surprise. "You scared me. What are you doing here? I thought we agreed to meet at the Bed and Breakfast."

"I changed my mind. Thought I'd pick you up before Conway knows you're missing." He laughed. "God, what I wouldn't give to see his face when he realizes."

Daniel took comfort from the weight of the loaded gun in his hand. He hoped the rookie cop covering Suzie had enough experience to keep her well out of the way—by whatever means necessary. He wanted to charge at Lowell but knew it would pay to bide his time just a little longer. He looked up when Lowell spoke again.

"You see, I knew Conway would insist on taking you back to his house after the things I said to him, Julia. The man is so predictable."

"What things?" Julia asked.

"None of that matters anymore. Look, whether or not you truly want to help me, I can't risk it. I'm leaving. The chances are the police will disregard your testimony and stick Derek's murder on me anyway."

"How can they? A woman shot Derek. They don't have any idea you were involved."

"But they must have, or why would you be so keen on seeing me? You really must think I was born yesterday to fall for your little charade of wanting me back. Oh, no, sorry, you don't want me back, do you? You just want us to be friends." He grinned. "Isn't that what you suggested?"

"You have to trust in the system, Marcus."

He snorted. "Oh, Julia. You expect me to believe you've suddenly had a complete change of heart about the police? Your brother was shot dead by one of them and you're preaching to me about justice? God, you should be ashamed."

Daniel heard her sharp intake of breath and pain burned deep in his chest. Lowell may as well have stuck a knife in her heart. He was goading her, hurting her and all the while she still had the same defiant tilt of her chin. Lowell was wrong. Daniel had already figured out why she was here, doing this, putting her own life in danger. There was no way Julia could allow Derek's murder to go unpunished. But to Daniel that meant, in turn, she didn't trust him to get the job done.

The pain in his chest intensified.

Marcus took a few steps closer to her and brushed the hair that had fallen from her ponytail back from her face. "I have to go before they find me. I've got myself into a mess I can see no way out of right now. But I will. I always do."

"Did you arrange for Derek to be killed, Marcus?" Julia asked, quietly.

Daniel's pulse beat rhythmically at his temple. *Confess it, you asshole. Confess it and then I've got you.*

"What did you say?" Marcus' voice was low, angry.

"I said, did you arrange for Derek to be killed?"

Lowell didn't answer and the two of them remained locked in a battle of wills that Daniel knew could explode at any minute. He lifted his gun. The atmosphere hung around them thick and suffocating. Marcus hadn't let go of her hair and now tightened it around his fingers. She gave a gasp.

"If I didn't know you better, Julia, I'd say you were trying to piss me off," he said. "Now why would you want to go and do a thing like that when you might never see me again?"

He wrenched a gun from the back of his pants and pushed her roughly to the ground.

Daniel snapped. Confessions and careful policing evaporated as he burst from his hiding place with a primitive roar and ran headlong at Lowell.

"Daniel! No!"

But Daniel ignored her yell and ran full speed toward Lowell. Lowell braced himself against Daniel's attack, but to little avail. Their groans and shouts echoed in the air as they tumbled to the muddy leaf-strewn ground. Daniel grunted as Lowell brought the butt of the gun down hard against his jaw. But the pain brought fresh determination and he pushed hard against Lowell's chest and heaved him to the side.

Before Lowell could catch his breath, Daniel was on top of him. He straddled Lowell and tried to extract the gun from his unyielding grip.

"Let it go," Daniel ordered. "I have back-up."

"Yeah, where are they then?" gasped, Lowell, still struggling.

"Right here."

Daniel, Marcus and Julia all turned to the sound of the young officer's voice, who had Suzie handcuffed beside him.

"Suzie? Oh, no," cried Julia. "Not you. It was you?"

"Oh, shut up, Julia. What the hell do you know?" Suzie sneered. "With your blonde good looks and fucking perfect figure. I did what I had to be done to get my man, OK?"

"You shot Derek for *him*? For Marcus?"

"Derek was so near to topping himself it didn't matter anyway. We had to make sure he didn't blab to the police about Marcus' loaning business."

"But Thelma. How could you do this to her?"

"Do what? She's in her eighties for God's sake. She would've been a widow sooner or later."

Daniel watched the rage spread over Julia's face as she processed the vile truth of the woman standing opposite her. Suddenly Julia lunged forward and slapped Suzie so hard across the face her head ricocheted backwards.

Lowell seized his chance and with an almighty roar, Daniel was catapulted through the air and rolling away over snapping twigs and bracken.

"Daniel!"

Daniel heard Julia's scream and scrambled to his feet. His breath rasped against his dry throat, his jaw throbbed from the blow of Lowell's gun butt, but it was nothing compared to the rage roaring through him when he saw Lowell had grabbed Julia and now the pair of them were on the ground. She pulled at his hair and kicked at him with frenzied ferocity.

Daniel took a step forward, but before he could reach them, Lowell punched Julia in the face and she toppled backward.

"You're finished, Lowell. Do you hear me?" Daniel bellowed, pointing his gun at him.

Marcus merely grinned. Blood showing black amongst his teeth, his eyes wild with fury. He raised his own gun but instead of pointing it at Daniel, swiveled around and pointed it at Julia.

"I don't think so, Inspector. You shoot me and it might just trigger my own gun."

Adrenaline pumped through Daniel's veins but all he could think about was Julia, watching another cop point a gun at yet another human being.

He glanced at her. Even then, in that terrifying moment she looked so beautiful in the half-light. His mind grappled with his choices. One might cause Julia's death, the other more trauma to someone who'd already been through far too much.

Two gunshots simultaneously rang out and for one stunned instant, Daniel thought he had made the choice and fired unconsciously. But no, he hadn't.

He saw, with horrific clarity, that one of the shots had come from Lowell's gun.

Epilogue

Julia struggled to open eyelids that felt as heavy as lead. She had no idea where she was. Everything was white and far too bright. Her eyes fluttered closed again. Sleep. She just needed to sleep. Her throat was dry and a horrible, medicinal smell hung in the air like air-borne chloroform.

"Hey, don't think I'm going to sit here another ten hours waiting for you to wake up, sleepy-head."

A soft smile curved her lips. Daniel. Her eyes flickered open once more and met his.

"Hi."

He smiled. "Hi yourself."

"Am I in the hospital? Or a really badly decorated bedroom?"

He laughed. "Hospital."

"He got me, didn't he?"

Daniel nodded before dropping his gaze to her hand, which he held tightly in his own. "I'm sorry."

"What for? Please tell me you got him."

"Of course I did. He's dead, Julia."

"Good."

He kissed her knuckles. "But the last thing I wanted was for you to see another cop shooting someone."

"Just as well I was unconscious then," she said simply. "What about Suzie? What will happen to her? Is she in prison?"

"She'll be held in custody until her trial. What she did for love was as bad as it gets. She'll get life, Julia. I'm sure of it."

"All that time, Daniel. All that time we spent

with her, talking to her. How could we have not seen it?"

"Let's not talk about it."

Julia took in the line of his jaw, the furrow in his brow and knew just what he was thinking. "Hey, look at me. Daniel. Please, look at me. You could not have known it was Suzie any more than I did. Never would I have suspected Suzie of being so callously involved in Marcus' plans. He was the one out of control." She closed her eyes against the stab of pain in her shoulder. "None of us could have guessed what she had done."

"You could've been killed," he said, running a gentle finger over her closed lids.

"But I wasn't."

She heard the sheets move and the bed lowered slightly under his weight as he sat down beside her. She sighed under the protective comfort of his arm as he placed it across her middle. She wished he could join her in the bed, but supposed that wouldn't do at all.

"I guess I let down my new employers on the Princess II after all," she muttered.

"After all?"

"I rang them a few days ago. I'd already decided leaving on that ship was the last thing I wanted to do."

"It was?"

She smiled to hear the surprised pleasure in his voice. "Of course it was."

"But after what you said to your Mom..."

She shook her head. "I love you and I was afraid..."

"Pardon?"

"I said, I love you and..."

"At last!"

He leaned forward, his lips warm against hers. And then they were on her jaw, her neck. She squeezed her thighs together to stem the automatic trembling there every time he touched her.

"Mmmm, I love you, Inspector Conway."

"Pardon? I didn't quite hear that."

She giggled as he nipped her. "I said, I love you!"

"I love you too, Miss Kershaw."

And then he kissed her, long and hard, all the while careful not to lean any weight on her although she yearned to feel his entire body pressed close to hers. Slowly, he drew back. She opened her eyes, to see him watching her.

"What is it?"

"Are you still afraid?"

She inhaled a shaky breath. "I'm worried about what my mother's going to say about us being together but..." She paused, held his cheek in her hand. "But the truth is before I met you my mother's grief as well as my own was more than I could cope with." She smiled tentatively. "But with you, I feel stronger. I'm going to make her see I love her, but she has to move on with her life. Phil will always be here, in our hearts and in our thoughts. She has to understand that."

"And once you do that, you think she'll accept you seeing a cop?"

"To me, you're Daniel—the cop part is your job. I know, if we give her time, she'll see you in the same way as I do, and love you just as much."

He pressed a kiss to her forehead. "I'm going to make you so happy."

Her smile bubbled into a full-fledged grin. "You'd better."

About the Author...

Reluctant Witness is my second book with the Wild Rose Press and I'm absolutely thrilled! I have gained in confidence and experience since my first release so I really hope my existing readers will enjoy this book even more and any new readers will want to go on to buy *Searching for Sophie*. I have just completed my first romantic comedy and soon hope to secure an agent. My husband and two children are as supportive as ever and I wouldn't know what to do without them. Happy reading!

Visit Rachel at www.rachelbrimble.com

Contact Rachel at:
Rachel.brimble@btinternet.com

Lightning Source UK Ltd.
Milton Keynes UK
14 January 2010
148571UK00001B/16/P